CHRISTM

ALSO BY JESSICA THORN

Rocky Point Romance Series
Second Chance Girl
Just My Luck (Coming 2021)

Pine Grove Romance Series
Christmas in Pine Grove

All Jessica Thorn's books can be read in Kindle Unlimited

Copyright © 2020 Jessica Thorn

All rights reserved. No part of this publication may be reproduced, distributed, or transmitted in any form or by any means, including photocopying, recording, or other electronic or mechanical methods, without the prior written permission of the publisher, except in the case of brief quotations embodied in critical reviews and certain other noncommercial uses permitted by copyright law.

Any references to historical events, real people, or real places are used fictitiously. Names, characters, and places are products of the author's imagination.

Front cover image by FrozenStar at
http://www.selfpubbookcovers.com/FrozenStar

Printed by Kindle Direct Publishing, in the United States of America.

First printing edition 2020.

JESSICA THORN

To my family, for always encouraging and supporting me
To my best friend, for always believing in me
And to my love, for inspiring me
Thank you

CHRISTMAS IN PINE GROVE
A Novel

Jessica Thorn

Chapter One

Something about the holiday season, all the sparkling lights, all the shiny red and green decor, all the glitter... something about it just gave Faye Parker a migraine. She didn't *hate* the holiday season. Nobody could *hate* the holidays. It just seemed like, more and more, the season of thankfulness and giving reminded her more of the things she didn't have than the things she did.

Continuing her slow stroll down the candy aisle at the local Stop & Save, the piercing tones of a child demanding a Hippopotamus for Christmas blaring from the overhead speakers, Faye perused the rows upon rows of chocolate Santa's, tree-shaped peanut butter cups, and candy canes. She snagged a box of peppermint bark off the shelf and placed it in her basket, then did the same with a bag of the peanut butter cup trees. Only three more weeks until Christmas, so she just needed enough candy to last her until then. On impulse, she grabbed a bag of multi-colored gumdrop candies off a shelf, inspected them for a moment, then tossed them into the basket, too, with the rest of her haul. Satisfied with the amount of sugar in her basket, she turned to head back toward the registers when the familiar glint of a red and silver tin caught her eye.

Faye beelined toward the box of Vreeland's Ribbon Candy, a mixture of excitement and nostalgia filling her to the brim. She picked it up with both hands, smoothing her thumbs over the shiny raised Christmas trees and snowmen that adorned the tin. For a moment, she wasn't standing in the candy aisle of the grocery store, but rather in her childhood kitchen, her grandmother having just handed her the tin of gorgeous, colorful, swirling candies, just like she did every year.

Unexpectedly, tears stung in her eyes. She wouldn't receive a box of ribbon candy this year.

Stupid, stupid holidays.

"I've always wondered how anyone could eat Ribbon Candy willingly. It's like asking for cavities."

Faye jumped, startled at the deep voice that had pulled her out of her memories. She whirled around to see a man standing behind her, arms folded over his chest, looking at her with one eyebrow cocked and a smirk tugging at the corner of his lips. She locked onto his deep brown eyes, and for a moment she forgot how to breathe.

"Eh...excuse me?" she asked after a moment, her brain finally kicking back into gear. She had to tear her eyes away from his face, but they just landed on a pair of broad shoulders that, even under his bulky winter jacket, Faye could tell were well-built. Not helpful.

"Cavities," he said, nodding at box of Ribbon Candy in her hand. "It's basically just straight sugar. But hey," he put his hands up in front of him. "Your teeth, your call."

She looked down and had to fight the wave of embarrassment that washed over. Who the hell was this guy? Defiantly, she turned to face him and carefully placed the tin into her basket.

"Maybe I will get cavities, maybe I won't. Can't see how it's any of your business."

Before he could respond, she turned around and headed to the frozen foods' aisle, and away from the random judgmental guy who apparently hated candy. Not that she wasn't flattered by random men striking up conversations with her in public, she just really wasn't in the mood after the day she'd had. Between the cold spreading through her second- grade classroom, causing grumpy kids and snot everywhere, and the mountain of homework assignments she had to grade, her sanity was hanging on by a thread. She just wanted to finish her grocery shopping, go home, crawl into bed, and call it a day.

She was browsing frozen microwave entrées when she felt a pair of eyes watching her. She ignored it at first, choosing instead to focus on whether she felt like chicken or pasta for dinner. Deciding either would go fine with a glass or four of red wine, she picked one at random and tossed it in her cart next to the gum drops. Still feeling like she was being watched, she moved down to the frozen vegetables to grab a few bags for the rare occasions she felt like actually cooking. After picking out a few mixed veggie bags, she turned around, and nearly crashed right into the guy from the candy aisle.

"Not much for cooking, are you?" he asked, peering into her cart and frowning. *Who is this guy?* she thought, the accusation making her feel defensive. She could cook! She was just busy. If she had unlimited free time, she would cook every meal from scratch. But she had assignments to grade, and lesson plans to write, and laundry creating a replica of Mount Everest in her bedroom. Her free time was already limited - she couldn't imagine spending it cooking.

Wanting to see just how much better than her this guy thought he was, she peered back into his cart, and frowned. A carton of eggs, a gallon of milk, a variety of fresh, colorful produce and a few wrapped packages of meat from the butcher counter stared back at her. Not a single piece of candy.

"Well, not all of us have the free time to cook gourmet meals," she said. "Some of us are very busy."

She peeled off down the aisle, the guy following alongside her. He didn't seem deterred by her dismissive attitude, and she found it supremely annoying.

"I love to cook," he said, as if she'd asked for his opinion. What had she done to deserve this? Was the universe punishing her? She made a mental note to go over anything that could have thrown the karmic scales off balance later.

"That's great for you," she said dryly, turning down the wine and beer aisle and stopping in front of the reds. She already had a bottle at home, but the way her week was going, she figured it couldn't hurt to have a few more.

"It could be great for you, too," he said. His forwardness caught her off guard, and caught her attention.

"Excuse me?" she said, turning to look at him. Her hand was frozen on a bottle of Pinot Noir, and she could feel her cheeks turning red and hot. He took a tiny step backward, and she was sure it was because she had murder in her eyes.

"Pinot's a great choice," he said, pointing to the wine in her hand. "I prefer a Malbec myself, but nothing beats sipping a glass of Pinot outside a little Brasserie in Burgundy, I'll give you that." Faye closed her eyes.

"What is your point?" she drew out each word, her patience growing thinner by the second.

He smiled, a dazzling, bright white smile that caused the corners of his eyes, the color of melted chocolate, to crinkle in delight. Her pulse quickened traitorously.

"I was thinking that I could cook you dinner some time," he said, taking a step closer to her. Apparently, her intimidating demeanor had worn off.

"Why on earth would I want to have dinner with you?" she asked, placing two bottles of the Pinot Noir in her cart, then facing him, crossing her arms in front of her. "You just spent the last five minutes insulting me."

"Because you need someone to cook you a real meal," he said, grimacing at the contents of her cart. "You can't just spend each night eating frozen dinners in front of the television. Where's the fun in that?"

There it is, she thought, shaking her head. He could quite possibly be the most arrogant human being on the planet.

"There you go again," she said, narrowing her eyes at him. "Do you actually think this works? Making me feel like I can't possibly be happy with my life the way it is if it doesn't include a man taking care of me? How long did it take for your ego to grow that big, anyway?"

"How long have you been too busy to make time for yourself?" he asked.

Her mouth dropped open. Was he serious? "None of your business."

"Okay then," he said. "What do you do for a living that keeps you so busy?"

"I'm a NASA engineer," she lied.

"That must be very challenging," he said.

"Apparently not as challenging as getting you to take a hint."

He tilted his head, that smirk returning.

"You really don't want to have dinner with me?" he asked. Faye couldn't help it, she burst out laughing.

"I don't even know you," she said, but he continued to look at her in disbelief. Exasperated, she threw up her hands. "Is it really so hard for you to believe that I don't want to have dinner with you?"

"It's hard to believe you'd rather eat frozen, microwave lasagna," he replied.

"Don't forget the Ribbon Candy. I'd definitely much rather break my teeth on that, than have dinner with you."

She pushed past him, ignoring the fact that his smile had grown ten times wider.

"Suit yourself!" he called after her.

She took one glance back, and was relieved to see he wasn't following her. Instead, he stood rooted in place, watching her leave. Their eyes met, and he winked at her.

"Ugh!" She swallowed, rolling her eyes so hard she risked pulling a muscle. How come the only men she attracted were always egotistical jerks? Maybe that was why she hadn't had an actual relationship in... well, a long time. She supposed she could add that to the list of things the holidays reminded her she was missing.

A few minutes later, Faye finished her shopping and floated through the checkout line, grateful for a few minutes of peace, but unable to keep from looking over her shoulder at the other shoppers around her. She hated that her cheeks still felt flushed, and she had to force herself not to think of the way candy aisle guy had flashed her that big, brilliant smile.

When she got out to her car, she caught a glimpse of someone walking to another car in the reflection of her driver's side window. She froze when she realized who it was.

"You've got to be kidding me," she muttered.

The guy from earlier was walking out of the store, a brown-paper shopping bag cradled in either arm. Faye eyed him as he strolled over to a sporty, red convertible BMW.

Figures.

He opened his driver's side door, looked up, and locked eyes with her. She froze and he just smile, tossing her a small wave, and then loaded the bags into the car, climbed in, and peeled out of the parking lot.

It was a good thing she'd picked up that extra bottle of wine because, oh boy, was she going to need it.

The next morning, Faye sat outside the Principal of Pine Grove Elementary's office, her leg bobbing nervously up and down. She'd come into an email from her boss asking her to meet him in his office before classes started, and she had no idea what to expect. It wasn't like him to be so cryptic, and she wondered what he could possibly need to talk to her about so urgently. She had been wracking her brain all morning since she'd received the email, wondering if she'd forgotten about parent-teacher conferences, or worrying that there was an issue with one of her students. After several more minutes of sitting in stressful silence, the door to his office creaked open, and a hand gestured her inside.

Inhaling a deep, steadying breath, she stood up and walked into the office, taking a seat opposite him at his large, oak desk.

"What can I do for you, Bob?" she asked, her eyes settling on the tie around her bosses rotund neck. It was red, and dotted with Christmas trees, and it stood out from her boss' otherwise drab gray jacket.

"I'll try to make this brief," Bob said, handing Faye a print-out of an email. A quick scan of the fancy signature at the bottom told her it came from the Superintendent of Schools, a fact which caused her stomach to drop like a boulder tumbling off a cliff. She dragged her eyes from the signature back to the top, and began to read.

Mr. Griffin,

As you well know, the town of Pine Grove is fortunate enough to be gaining a new, rather notable resident. Dylan Andersen, celebrated snowboarder, and X-games competitor, is expected to not just contribute greatly to the town, but to the Pine Grove school district as well.

Her head snapped up, her mouth agape.

"Pine Grove is getting a... *celebrity*?" she asked. Bob nodded, biting his nails and avoiding eye contact.

She read the next part out loud. "Not only will he be an esteemed member of the community, but he will also be contributing *$50,000 to the school district's winter sports program,* in an effort to educate kids on ways to stay active during the cold winter months."

Faye put the paper down, her eyes wide. "$50,000?" she asked. "To what, teach kids how to ski?"

"Well, it's really more than that," Bob said, his tone and expression suddenly light. "It's going toward health education, as well, and I believe some of the funds have been cleared for use in other sports programs." His face darkened again. "Please, keep going."

She snatched up the paper again, and continued reading out loud.

"In order to repay his generosity, we have decided to grant him the following requests made in regard to his son's education." She paused again, a sudden chill coming over her. She glanced up at Bob, nervous to continue reading, but he urged her on.

"One -" she read, "Mr. Andersen will be granted weekly meetings with his son's teacher to develop goals, discuss his son's progress, and address any obstacles to his son's success." *This is second grade*, she thought sardonically, but continued. "Two - Outside of these meetings, any issues, academic or otherwise, concerning Mr. Andersen's son will be brought to the attention of Mr. Andersen via email or phone call immediately. Three- Mr. Andersen reserves the right to attend his son's class at any time and *participate when necessary*?"

Faye slapped the paper down on Bob's desk, her mouth agape as she tried to process what she'd just read. Bob jumped a little in his seat, but kept his hands folded neatly in front of him as he waited for Faye to speak.

"This can't be serious," she said, feeling a laugh welling up inside of her. "These *'requests'* are insane. What would he need to participate in class for?"

"Well," Bob said, trying to keep a light tone but avoiding Faye's eyes like she might turn him to stone. "According to the Superintendent, Mr. Andersen's son has been privately tutored up until this point, and Mr. Andersen has been very involved in his education. While he's excited for his son to experience 'real school'...," Bob made air quotes around the words "real school," and that made Faye inexplicably angry, "he is concerned about the quality of his son's education."

Faye clenched her teeth so hard, she felt a migraine coming on.

"He's a two-time Olympic gold-medalist, whoop-de-freaking-doo!" Faye protested. "It's not like he's Ben Affleck or something!"

Bob shifted uncomfortably in his chair, clearing his throat, and tugging at the starched white collar around his rotund neck. Faye stood up and paced Bob's small but cozy office, arms crossed tightly across her chest. It had been freezing this morning when she left the house, barely twenty degrees and starting to flurry, so she'd chosen to wear a thick cashmere sweater. Now, the material felt stuffy and too hot, like it was holding her hostage.

"I'm sure he means well..." Bob started to say, but Faye wrung her hands in front of her.

"I'm an *awesome* teacher, ask anybody!" she said. "Does he think I won't be good enough?" She rolled up her sleeves and turned to look at her boss. She watched him shift a little in his chair as she loomed over his desk, sweat beading at his gray, receded hairline.

Faye closed her eyes and sucked in a deep breath. She knew she was getting way too defensive, and needed to chill out. At 28 years old, she might have been the youngest teacher in Pine Grove, but that didn't mean she wasn't experienced. Pine Grove was a small town, and growing up there meant that, not only had she been a student of the great Pine Grove SD herself, but she knew all the families and children that passed through, as well. She'd commuted to the local university for college, and even done her student teaching at Pine Grove elementary. Faye lived and breathed this town and this school; everyone could see that. She opened her eyes and exhaled slowly.

"All I'm saying," she said calmly, retreating into one of the stiff wooden chairs opposite Bob and clasping her hands, "is that I'm a good teacher. I'm passionate about my students, and this town, and I'm just as capable as some fancy private tutor. Better, even."

"I'm not saying you aren't, but Dylan Andersen doesn't know any of that. He doesn't know this town; he doesn't know you or your story. He doesn't know that you're one of the best teachers in Pine Grove, *or* the state of New York. But he *will*, Faye. This is just a... a game we have to play for a little while."

Faye stood up again, unable to sit still, and began to pace once more. "It's not even me I'm really worried about," she continued. "It's the students. Imagine what a distraction it will be having a pro snowboarder hanging around the classroom. The kids won't be able to focus, I'll be competing for their attention... not to mention the fact that his poor son will be in the spotlight from the moment he walks through those doors."

Bob nodded, his face solemn. Faye knew she was preaching to the choir, but also understood that there was more at play here than just someone knew moving into town. Bob seemed to read her mind.

"It's just for a short while," Bob said. "But, you read that email, Faye, this is more political than anything. He's made a sizable donation to the school district, and this is the school's end of the bargain. We have to play by these rules, there's nothing to be done."

Faye nodded, trying to appear understanding despite the growing knot in her stomach. "Well, I'll do whatever needs doing," she said. She felt exhausted, all of a sudden. She looked at the clock above Bob's office door, and realized there was only ten minutes left until class was set to begin. "I better be getting back," she said.

She turned to leave, and cringed when she heard Bob clear his throat.

"There's just one more thing," Bob said. Slowly, Faye turned back to face him, wondering what else Bob could possibly add to the already nonsensical situation. "He is requesting a meeting with you and I tomorrow afternoon, after classes let out. His son is already enrolled, but he wants to meet his teacher before he starts."

"Of course," Faye said, gritting her teeth. In her head, it had sounded like, *Of course he does! Why wouldn't he?,* but she was glad what had actually come out of her mouth had been a little more civilized.

"Alright then," Bob said. "Well, try not to worry too much about it. We'll reconvene tomorrow before the meeting."

"Great," she said sharply, and without another word, disappeared out of Bob's office.

It was most certainly *not* great, but what could she do? She decided to try and put it out of her mind for the time being, instead focusing on the day's lesson plan. Hopefully, her dedication would speak for itself. *Hopefully.*

Chapter Two

"Daddy, can we go to the lake?"

"Lake's frozen, Benny."

The little boy pouted, his bottom lip quivering. Dylan's heart ached for him, knowing it would take some time to adjust to their new home. Ben tried to cross his arms over his chest, a gesture of his unhappiness at the frozen lake situation, but his hyper-insulated winter coat was too thick. This made him pout even more, and Dylan saw tears beginning to well up in his sweet seven-year-old's eyes. He ruffled the boy's dirty blond curls– nothing like his own dark hair – and this earned him a small, brief smile.

"We can take the canoe out as soon as Spring comes, and everything thaws out," Dylan said. "And hey, maybe there's ice skating."

The prospect of ice skating seemed to distract Ben a little, his frown dissipating. The pair were strolling through the small but bustling Pine Grove village center, trying their best to acclimate to their new home. They'd walked by the post office, where Ben had wanted to check out the "big white trucks," had stopped for a hot chocolate at the local coffee shop, and were now taking a quick stroll by Ben's new elementary school. The sudden reminder that his son would soon be attending public school, that his little boy would be away from him for seven hours a day, tugged at Dylan's heart.

Ben was so excited about attending "real school," as he called it, though Dylan often pointed out he had always been attending "real school," just on the road. Ben had always had a private instructor, someone who at first traveled with them to the various competitions and Olympic training exercises Dylan attended, and as Ben got older, a remote teacher who could connect with Ben anywhere via a computer and an internet connection. Ben was most excited about the other students, though. "I'll get to raise my hand in class, dad," he'd said, "and I won't always be the one answering the teacher's questions. I want a lunch buddy. Do you think you get to pick those?"

Those moments with Ben- the excitement in his eyes at the prospect of making friends and having a lunch buddy, of having to raise his hand in class to answer a question- reminded Dylan of why they were doing this, of why this was so important. Sure, there was Dylan's knee injury, and abrupt end to his professional snowboarding career. Without the competition or the prospect of another Olympics on the horizon, they no longer needed to travel so much and settling down in one place was the most logical decision. Plus, despite months of recovery, he still wasn't fully healed. But this change also made the most sense for Ben, who at seven would be hitting social and developmental milestones that could be crippled by the transient and isolated life of being "on the road."

Dylan knew that better than anyone.

They could very well have settled down in Los Angeles with Dylan's parents, but Dylan wanted to give Ben a normal childhood, or at least as close as he could come to it. And his parents were... extravagant. There would be prep schools and country clubs and too much social pressure, and Dylan didn't want that for his son. When his buddy from his X-Games days, Marcus, had told him about Pine Grove, it had seemed like just the right amount of normal. Marcus had nothing but praise for the small town in rural, up-state New York that he'd grown up in, boring him with tales of Spring festivals and community sports leagues and rallies for the high school's football games. But boring was good. Boring was exactly what they'd needed.

It didn't take long to find a house, and Dylan wasn't exactly hurting for money. He'd settled on a fixer-upper, one with good bones that was structurally sound, but that needed a fair amount of upgrading and TLC. He wanted to do most of the work himself, partly to keep himself busy but also to make the house *theirs*. He had plans to start a new career, maybe open his own business, but for now settling Ben in was priority number one. Marcus was helpful throughout the process, pulling out his connections in the community to find Dylan a good real estate agent, a team of guys to help them move, and a banker at the local credit union ready to talk business loans whenever Dylan was ready. They had hardly been moved in a few days when casseroles and plates of cookies and cakes started showing up on his porch. The mysteries of small town life had always alluded Dylan, who'd spent his youth on the road and any consecutive time in one place in a major city. He liked it, though. He liked feeling a part of something.

"Do I get to meet my teacher today, too, dad?" Ben asked.

"Not today, buddy. You will soon, though."

Ben pouted again, but recovered quickly. He knew it was probably stupid to want to scope out the school and Ben's teacher before Ben's first day, but something inside him needed to be absolutely sure that this was right for Ben. Pine Grove's school district was highly rated, not to mention there wasn't a private school for miles. But perhaps if Dylan could tour the school, assess the teacher he'd been assigned, make sure they were the absolute right fit for his son, maybe he'd feel a little better about it. Or maybe he could convince Ben's tutor to move to New York…

He sighed aloud to himself, Ben paying him no mind. *Probably not.*

They made their way back through the village now, and Dylan had to pause to admire the scenery. Poplar trees lined Main Street, which was buffered by a myriad of shops and restaurants on one side, a shimmering glacial lake on the other. Dylan had heard that the lake's water was so clean, it served as the town's primary source of fresh water. They walked past Brigsby's Books, Lakeside Cycle Shop, and several other small, boutique shops toward Marcus' parents' house. Marcus wouldn't be there, of course. He was in Aspen, working on getting more sponsorships for the next X-Games and next year's Winter Olympics. Marcus had enlisted his sister, Iris, to help Dylan and Ben get settled and to watch Ben if Dylan needed a sitter. Iris, a sunny 24-year-old, lived at home and worked a handful of part time jobs to pay for community college classes. Marcus had told Dylan how he'd begged her to let him pay for her college, anywhere she wanted, and she'd downright refused. She wanted to do it all on her own, pay her own way, and make something of herself. When Dylan called her about watching Ben this afternoon, she'd been happy to do it, saying she was always looking for ways to fill up her free time. They were planning to meet with Iris now, and let Ben spend an hour getting to know her while Dylan went for a brief doctor's appointment. He shuddered at the thought of leaving Ben, wondering if moving to Pine Grove- and all the changes that came with it- would be more of an adjustment for Ben, or for himself.

"Do you think Iris will like me?" Ben asked as they continued walking, taking a right down Primrose Street and heading away from the lake and Village proper. They passed perfectly manicured lawns prefacing well-kept Craftsman's and Victorians, Dylan counting the house numbers as he looked for Marcus' family home.

"Of course she will!" Dylan responded, crouching down in front of his son. "You're the best kid I know. Now, I'm going to need your help finding their house. Can you tell me when you see it? It's number 242, and it has a big, *yellow,* door."

Ben nodded excitedly, taking off down the quiet street in search of the house. Dylan exhaled sharply as he rose from his crouching position, wincing in pain. Slowly, he ambled after Ben, hoping his knee would hold out until he could make it to his doctor's appointment.

"I found it! It's here!" Ben exclaimed, jumping up and down and pointing toward the yellow front door. Dylan followed as Ben hurried up the walkway and knocked on the front door, the smile on his son's face telling him everything he needed to know about whether this was the right place for them.

HALF AN HOUR LATER, after Ben and Iris had been introduced and Dylan had gotten to catch up with his best friend's little sister, Dylan found himself in the sterile, utilitarian waiting room of Pine Grove's singular practicing Orthopedic specialist. Dylan doubted that Dr. Bryce McCann had ever treated a professional athlete before, but then, most hadn't. He'd used a well-known Orthopedic surgeon based out of Los Angeles that his parents recommended right after he'd gotten hurt. The surgeon had boasted about rehabbing celebrity stuntmen and various NFL players, and Dylan had felt in competent - if conceited - hands. After that, he'd floated between appointments with an assigned Orthopedist and Physical Therapist from the National Olympic Committee. Later, when he'd announced his retirement from the sport of professional Snowboarding, those doctors who had been so eager to treat him suddenly had less and less open appointment slots, if any at all.

Dylan wanted to avoid having to travel for check-ups and Cortisone shots, and figured he'd give the town's local physician a try. Looking around the empty waiting room at the faded posters proclaiming, "Cover your Cough!" and the importance of the acronym R.I.C.E., Dylan felt increasingly uneasy. A tiny, Charlie Brown-like Christmas tree sat pitifully atop a wooden end table, failing to bring any semblance of Christmas cheer to the office. He needed to be 100%, and he just hoped this doctor would be able to get him there.

"Mr. Andersen?" squeaked the stout woman behind the counter where he'd checked in. He got up, and watched her adjust her big, round glasses and smooth her wispy silver curls, all the while beaming at him. "Dr. McCann will see you now," she said. "You can come on back."

He did as he was told, leaving the waiting room through a tan, nondescript door that lead back to the patient rooms. The woman waited in the hallway for him, looking him up and down as he walked toward her. "This is very exciting," she giggled. "We don't ever get celebrities around here." He followed her back past several empty rooms, until they reached a door with a big number 4 on it, and she gestured him inside. "The doctor will be in to see you shortly, you're in good hands," she said.

Dylan smiled.

"Thank you," he said. The woman lingered in the doorway, still beaming at him.

"I'm Doris, by the way," she said, extending her hand out. "You just give me a holler if you need anything."

Dylan shook her hand, and the woman blushed profusely. "Thanks Doris, I appreciate it."

Doris tittered all the way out of the room, leaving him to hang up his jacket and wait for the doctor in silence. After a few minutes, there was a light knock on the door, and in stepped Doctor McCann.

The doctor was much, much younger than Dylan had expected. He looked to be no more than mid-thirties, and while Dylan thought this should make him uneasy, it didn't. In fact, he actually felt a little more comfortable. Doctor McCann thrust out his hand toward Dylan, and they shook hands.

"Great to meet you, Mr. Andersen. I'd say I'm a huge fan, but I must admit, I'm not much of a snowboarder," the doctor said. Much to Dylan's surprise again, the admission made him all the more comfortable with the doctor. He realized it was probably the first time since moving to Pine Grove that he'd met someone who viewed him as a person first, pro-athlete second.

"Now, your last specialist and physical therapist both faxed over your medical history. You had quite the tear in your meniscus, I'm surprised they didn't recommend surgery initially," Doctor McCann said, scanning through several sheets of paper on a clipboard.

"My manager begged them not to, unless it was absolutely necessary," Dylan said. He wanted me back in the game as quickly as possible, and didn't want the rumor mills churning with stories of me being laid up in the hospital. He was worried it would negatively impact my sponsorships."

"What about how it would impact your ability to walk? With all due respect, Mr. Andersen, there is still considerable inflammation, and you've noted you still frequently experience pain. By this point, I would expect the inflammation to be minimal with proper healing. These results," Doctor McCann held up his clipboard for emphasis, giving Dylan a pointed look, "concern me."

Dylan heard the doctor loud and clear. He'd been willing to undergo surgical repair but Martin, his manager, had been adamant about maintaining Dylan's image for the sake of his sponsorships. He had let Martin talk him in to letting his knee "heal on its own," all while making press appearances to talk about how his injury was "no big deal," and he'd be back on the slopes in no time. After giving the same story over and over again in interviews, Dylan began to realize it just wasn't the truth. His downtime had given him the ability to reflect on his life and his future, and concluded that none of it was right for his son. What if he got hurt even worse next time? God forbid, what if he died? Who would Ben have? His snowboarding career was over, and that realization didn't even hurt that bad. His manager was the one truly broken up over it, and it took Dylan moving to some small rural town in New York to convince Martin that it was all over.

"Can you give me a shot for the pain, doc? I've been getting regular Cortisone injections to help ease the inflammation," Dylan said, massaging his knee. Doctor McCann just laughed and shook his head.

"I can give you a shot, but I have to stress that this is not a permanent solution. In fact, giving you the shot and allowing you walk around on it might just exacerbate the issue," Doctor McCann said.

"I'll take it easy," Dylan said. "Besides, I'm out of the game now anyway."

"And thank goodness for that," Doctor McCann said. "Take it from someone who knows - forcing your body to continue doing something like that, playing through injuries, it doesn't do you any favors in the long run."

That took Dylan by surprise.

"Sounds like you have some experience putting the sport before your health," Dylan said, thinking he might have judged Dr. McCann too quickly. The doctor grabbed a stool from underneath the counter in the room, placed it in front of Dylan, and sat down.

"I played football at Cal Poly for two years before I tore my rotator cuff in a bad tackle," Dr. McCann said. "My sophomore year, I was starting Running Back. I had a full ride on a football scholarship, and no plans beyond playing in the NFL. I went to class purely to get a passing grade so I could keep playing football. Then, I got injured."

"What happened after you got hurt?"

"I lost my scholarship the following year. Professional football was no longer an option," Dr. McCann said.

"What did you do?" Dylan asked, fully bought into the doctor's story.

"I had to pivot," Dr. McCann said. "I either had to take out loans and get serious about school, or I had to drop out. I did a lot of soul-searching, but eventually figured out that I could take my passion for sports and turn it into a living outside of professional football. I changed my major to biology, buckled down, and that eventually turned into Pre-Med. Pre-Med turned into medical school, which turned into a specialization in Orthopedic and Sports Medicine, and..." he gestured to the room around him, "here I am."

Dylan let that sink in for a moment. Surely, if Dr. McCann could change course as a teenager, Dylan could figure out what to do with himself at 32 years old. He suddenly felt more at ease than he had since leaving snowboarding, knowing his lack of direction couldn't possibly last forever. Plus, he now realized he had an ally in Dr. McCann, someone who knew exactly what he was going through. Even with all their experience, he couldn't say that about any of his previous Olympics-approved physicians.

Dr. McCann stood up and went to the cabinet behind him, pulling out a large syringe. Dylan shuddered at the sight of the enormous needle, and sucked in a deep breath. He despised getting any sort of injection, but knew it was the only thing that would calm the swelling in his knee and ease the pain. Once he was finished giving the injection, Dr. McCann took out a pen, scrawled something on a piece of paper from his clipboard, and then handed it to Dylan.

"It's a prescription for an anti-inflammatory that should ease the pain better than regular Ibuprofen," he said. "It may take a few days to feel the effects of the Cortisone, but even when it starts working, I want you to take it easy."

"Yes, doc," Dylan said.

"And I want to see you back here in a few weeks. If you're still having severe pain, I might recommend some Outpatient physical therapy," Dr. McCann added. "But I want you to try really resting it, first. I mean it."

"I will," Dylan said, putting a hand to his heart. "Scouts honor."

He shook the doctor's hand again, then headed back to Iris' house to pick up Ben. His mind raced as he thought about all the different directions he could go with his life, now that he didn't have the weight of sponsorships and competitions hanging over him. Dr. McCann's story had been unexpected, but it had inspired him. Once he and Ben were settled in, he was going to turn over a completely new leaf.

Chapter Three

Faye paced back and forth in her classroom, frantically scrutinizing every inch to make sure it looked presentable. She stopped to question what 'presentable' even meant in a classroom, especially one that housed 16 curious and rambunctious 2nd-graders. Her desks were lined up in four neat rows, facing her desk and the classroom's large chalkboard. To the right of the desks, next to the door, were cubbies where the children could set their backpacks and coats. To the left, under the classroom's large windows, were bookshelves full of chapter books that Faye liked to call her "little library." She encouraged the children to pick out a book to read during lunch, and often let them take it home to finish it when they asked. Next to the bookshelves were more cubbies, most full of supplies for arts and crafts, as well as extra school supplies. The walls were full of colorful posters, and a large banner hung above the chalkboard that read "Welcome to Second Grade!" She'd hung stockings on the cubby wall, one for each of her students, dangled snowflakes from the ceiling, and the door to her classroom was wrapped in Christmas wrapping paper like a giant present, complete with a big red bow.

Faye accepted that the classroom looked as good as it possibly could. It was Friday, and nobody looked forward to the weekend more than a group of seven-and-eight-year-olds who had been stuck at their desks all week and just wanted to play. The room typically looked like a tornado had blown through by 3 PM, so she'd done all she could. Taking a deep breath, she tried to calm her nerves, reminding herself of her abilities as an educator. She had to believe that Bob would have her back if the quality of her teaching was questioned. She had the backing and trust of the entire town, and she wasn't about to let one entitled celebrity ruin the respect and good reputation she'd worked so hard to build.

A knock on the door made her jump, and she braced herself for the impending discussion. She'd rehearsed the answers to every question she thought Dylan Andersen could possibly ask her a thousand times. She was ready.

The door swung open and Bob appeared in her doorway, his face flushed red and a large grin spread across it. Faye rolled her eyes at the obviously starstruck man. She was beginning to wonder if she was the only person in town *not* dazzled by Dylan Andersen. Bob entered and then, so did the newest member of the Pine Grove community.

Faye's brain went blank.

The man who'd entered into her classroom behind Principal Griffin was tall, at least 6'3", dwarfing both her and Bob. He wore a dark blue Calvin Klein sweater that fit tautly over his broad chest and shoulders, drawing her eyes from there down to light-wash jeans that hugged slim hips. She didn't know what she had expected, but it wasn't the man standing in front of her. She hadn't paid much attention to the famed Dylan Andersen on television – she wasn't really into watching sports or the Olympics – but she'd thought that snowboarders tended to be shorter. A *center-of-gravity* thing, or something. When she *had* seen him on TV, he'd always been bundled up in snow gear, with a hat and goggles obscuring his face. Today, he was just wearing sunglasses on his face, but as he stepped into the room, he removed them, and Faye suddenly felt like she might pass out. A pair of dark brown eyes stared back at her, glinting with mischief, the corners of his mouth drawn upward in a knowing smirk.

"*You!*" Faye gasped, gripping the desk as if suddenly, it was the only thing keeping her upright. Grocery store guy. The man who'd managed to insult her *and* ask her out in the same sentence. The man who'd criticized the items in her shopping basket, of all things. The man who bought a bunch of fresh vegetables and not a single frozen dinner, which she now realized was probably because he had a private chef to do all his cooking for him. *Dylan Andersen,* she thought, wondering if she had smoke coming out of her ears, because she was fuming. *Why am I not surprised?* she wondered. Startled, yes, but not surprised. He certainly fit the bill for the famous Playboy athlete reputation that preceded him. The smirk on Dylan's face widened into a full-blown smile, while Bob turned a deep shade of maroon. He looked from Faye, to Dylan, and then back to Faye, sweat beading on his hairline.

"Do you... do you two know each other?" he asked, tugging on the starched collar of his shirt.

"No!" Faye shouted, a little *too* quickly. Dylan just chuckled, which infuriated her.

Bob exhaled slowly, then turned to face him.

"Mr. Andersen, this is Faye Parker," he gestured to Faye, his voice wary, and edged with confusion. "She'll be Ben's teacher for the rest of this year."

Dylan reached out a large hand, his eyes locked on hers. Faye swallowed hard and reached out her hand, trying not to focus on the warmth spreading toward her fingertips as his hand engulfed hers. The handshake was cordial, but it sent a lightning bolt of heat down her arm. She struggled to form a coherent sentence.

"Nice to meet you," she managed, noting her voice sounded anything but delighted to be seeing the man in front of her again. She was close enough that she could see just how thick the lashes framing his eyes were. She could smell the sharp, masculine scent of his cologne, and it overwhelmed her. Why did she feel lightheaded all of a sudden? "I'm confident Pine Grove Elementary will be an excellent fit for your son."

Get it together, she told herself, wanting to put the brakes on her reaction to the man before she made an absolute fool out of herself. Besides, she knew his type – cocky, used to getting what he wants, can't take no for answer... Bob had made the stakes here clear, so she needed this to go well. And she most certainly was *not* about to feed his over-inflated ego.

"Well, that's what we're here to determine. Shall we get started?" Dylan said.

"Of course," Bob said. He gestured to two chairs in front of Faye's desk for him and Dylan - the only other two adult chairs in the room- and they all took a seat.

Faye had prepared her sermon. She took a deep breath and began. "Mr. Andersen," she said, "since 1907, Pine Grove Elementary has churned out bright young minds who go on to do amazing..."

"Ms. Parker," Dylan interrupted. "Principal Griffin. With all due respect, I'm sure that Pine Grove is a wonderful school."

Faye could sense a 'but' coming on. She shifted in her seat, trying to put on the same authoritative front she used with her students when they were being disruptive. Even sitting, though, Dylan seemed to tower over her. She didn't feel very much like the authority in the room.

"But," Dylan continued, "my son is a unique case. I doubt many of your students have come from the personalized, one-on-one style of learning he's had. I just want to be sure his education won't suffer by changing to a public-school environment."

"I assure you, Mr. Andersen, I've taught students from a variety of backgrounds," Faye countered. Bob looked from Faye, to Dylan, and back to Faye, his face red. His mouth hung slightly agape, as though he wanted to say something, but couldn't find the words.

"How long have you been teaching, Miss Parker?" Dylan asked. Faye felt her face get hot and her ears started to burn. In a matter of moments, he'd gone from friendly and flirty, to deadly serious. *Dr. Jekyll, anyone?* she thought. *You can have Mr. Hyde back now.*

"Six years," she answered, unsure what her tenure had to do with anything.

"And how many of those six years have been spent in the same school?" Dylan pressed.

"Well, I've... I've been at Pine Grove Elementary my whole career," Faye replied.

"Miss Parker is a skilled teacher," Bob chimed in, his voice frog-like, as if it had gotten stuck in his throat. "I can assure you of that."

"I don't doubt it, but I'm concerned that she has a lack of diverse experience," Dylan said. He turned to Faye, who was finding it more and more difficult to maintain her composure. Had Bob already discussed her work history with him? Dylan continued, "It's nothing personal, Ben is just used to a level of experience that I'm not sure someone who's spent their whole life in one place possesses."

Faye folded her hands in her lap, trying to maintain her composure. "I may not have spent my whole life traveling the world, and I know I haven't spent the last six years as a traveling private tutor, but I make a difference in this community," Faye said, her tone even but icy.

"And I was more than qualified to be in my first Olympics, but that didn't mean my team assumed I'd bring home the gold," Dylan said.

"With all due respect, I don't think this is the same thing at all," Faye seethed, her hands clenched into fists beside her.

"I agree," Dylan said, folding his arms across his chest. "I take my son's education much more seriously."

THE DEEP RED THAT FLARED all over the pale, delicate skin of Miss Parker's face and neck caused Dylan to grin like an absolute fool. He felt ashamed that he almost enjoyed getting a rise out of the woman before him. He truly was concerned about Ben and the quality of his education, but he'd also found her defensiveness... adorable. Her reaction to him had only fueled his fire. He found himself wanting to watch her cheeks flush with color, her mesmerizing green eyes narrow at him, her perfect pink lips purse in frustration. Dylan didn't think he'd ever enjoyed annoying someone so much.

"Miss Parker, if we could just lower our voice..." Bob made a downward pushing motion with both hands, like he often did to students in the hallways, but the sentiment was lost. Dylan stood up and leaned over the desk, getting eye-level with Faye. He had to contain the smirk tugging at the corner of his mouth as he watched her eyes widen, the tight line of her mouth quirking ever so slightly.

"I just want what's best for my son," he said, trying to mimic the irritation in her voice. They stared each other down for what felt like an eternity, eyes narrowed, and he would have been happy to stand there staring at her forever. Bob tried again to intervene.

"Perhaps we should take a short break?" he squeaked. "Get a cup of coffee?"

They ignored the suggestion.

"I'm sure you're used to getting what you want," Faye said, "but a gold medal can only get you so far in a small town. Word travels fast around here, and you wouldn't want anyone to judge you before they've had a chance to experience your sparkling personality for themselves."

"What's that supposed to mean?" Dylan asked. Her assertion jarred him, and he wondered if he'd been so focused on her pretty face, that he missed a chunk of their conversation. How had they gone from talking about Ben's education to his Olympic record? "We're not discussing me; we're discussing my son. How many gold medals I've won has nothing to do with it."

"We're a small school, Mr. Andersen. We have budgets, and limited resources. There are only two second grade teachers, and my class is the only one with room to accommodate another student. Your child is coming into school more than halfway through the first semester. He *could* go into the other class, but it would mean one of those students would need to be transferred into mine. They would be uprooted from the routine they've established and the friends they've made midway through the year to accommodate that. The school board may very well approve such a thing, but only because you've donated a large sum of money to the district's sports program," Faye explained. Dylan swore he could see her pulse throbbing in her throat, and briefly wondered what it would feel like to graze his lips across that spot. The vitriol in her voice, however, kept him rooted in reality. "So yes, your medals have everything to do with it."

He retreated a little, standing a few inches back from the desk. He watched her drop her eyes to the floor, inhaling a deep breath, as if her speech had taken all of her energy. Bob stood up, too, glaring at Faye and smoothing back his thin, gray hair. Dylan didn't look away from her, feeling a knot form in the pit of his stomach. She was something, and the part of him that had felt that lightning bolt of attraction when they'd first met wanted nothing more than to peddle back everything he'd just said. The pleasure he'd taken in getting under her skin morphed into a sudden desire to comfort her. He decided he wouldn't prolong her suffering any further for the day.

"Well, I think I've heard everything I need to hear," Dylan said, shrugging on his jacket and heading for the door. Bob jumped out of his seat and stumbled toward the door behind him. Sweat glistened on his brow, and Dylan noticed his face had become bright red and blotchy.

"About your, requests..." Bob said.

"What about them?" Dylan asked.

"Miss Parker would be more than happy to accommodate all of them," Bob said, nodding avidly. Dylan couldn't help but notice he looked like a bobble head. "And truly, Mr. Andersen, I think you'll find Pine Grove to be the perfect place to settle down, especially this time of year! You can almost count on a white Christmas in this part of New York, and we have this annual Holiday Festival that always draws a crowd. It's truly magical!"

"That's great news," Dylan said, addressing Faye. "I'll be sitting in on his first day, just to make sure everything is-" he emphasized the next words, practically begging her to react, "*up to par.*"

She scowled. *Mission accomplished,* he thought.

"Maybe you'll learn a thing or two," she muttered through gritted teeth. While Bob's face contorted into a look of pure horror, Dylan flashed her a grin and winked.

"I hope so, Miss Parker. I hope so."

Chapter Four

Whenever Faye was feeling the pressure, there was one thing she could always count on to make her feel better: *coffee.*

So, when a cappuccino appeared in front of Faye, all steamy and warm and calling her name, she reached for it. Just as she was about to wrap her fingers around the mug, though, it was yanked backward out of her reach. The villain on the other end of the mug was Chloe Monroe, owner of Chloe's Coffeehouse and Faye's closest friend in Pine Grove.

"Cruel and unusual punishment," Faye grumbled, pouting at her friend. Chloe smiled a devious smile and teased Faye with the cappuccino again.

"You can have coffee when you spill the beans," she said. "No pun intended."

"What is there to tell?" Faye asked, shifting in her stool at one of the cafe's high-top tables. "Our new celebrity resident thinks I'm too inexperienced to teach his son, and I have to let him sit in on my classes to prove him otherwise. It's like I'm on probation or something." She relayed to Chloe all of Dylan Andersen's requests, and how she'd unknowingly encountered him and his over-sized ego.

Chloe squeezed Faye's arm sympathetically, and then mercifully handed over the mug. Faye sipped and sighed. She often came to the café to work on lesson planning, or to grade tests. She liked the atmosphere, not to mention the coffee. Plus, Chloe had been her best friend since kindergarten.

"So, is he as cute in person as he is on TV?" Chloe asked, sitting down across from Faye and looking at her expectantly. The glint in her eyes, paired with her blond braided pigtails and smattering of freckles, made her look like a teenager waiting to be filled in on the latest gossip. Faye rolled her eyes, but she could feel the blush in her cheeks betraying her.

"Don't be gross," Faye snapped. "He's the enemy!"

"You're right, I'm sorry. He's a troll," Chloe cooed. Faye's stomach knotted even more.

"He's not, though," she whined, cradling her head in her hands. Chloe swatted at her.

"I can think of worse things than having to spend time with an Olympic athlete," she said. "At least you'll get a little eye candy in your day. I'm sure once he realizes how unnecessary his helicopter parenting is, he'll back off."

"He's going to be a distraction," Faye said, taking another long draw from her cup. "Not just to the kids, but to the other teachers, too! I don't want a bunch of groupies hanging around my classroom door every day, I have students to teach!"

"Give him ground rules," Chloe offered. "Make him sit in the corner quietly."

"I'm just going to be under a microscope now," Faye continued, ignoring her friend's attempts at lightening the mood. "I feel like the other teachers are all talking about it. I'll look like an absolute idiot if for some reason he decides to pull his son from my class."

"Who cares what everyone else thinks," Chloe said. "Besides, once he sees how good of a teacher you are, he'll probably call off the chaperoning and weekly check-ins anyway."

"Hopefully," Faye said. "Hopefully, I don't lose my sanity before then."

Chloe shot her a devious grin.

"You know, you *are* at a distinct advantage compared to the rest of the eligible women in this town," Chloe said. "And I've been telling you, you need a man in your life."

Faye froze, holding her cup in mid-air and staring wide-eyed at Chloe, who burst out laughing.

"What?" Chloe giggled.

"That is the last thing I need," Faye grumbled. And she meant it. "The last time I had anything resembling a relationship, it was a total disaster."

"That's a little dramatic, don't you think?" Chloe asked. Faye shook her head.

"Nope. We're talking Chernobyl-sized disaster."

Chloe's brows knitted together, her girlish grin contorting into a confused and concerned frown. She leaned back in her chair and crossed her arms, while Faye sipped quietly on her cappuccino.

"I thought you were over Peter?" Chloe asked.

"What? Of course I am," Faye snapped, refusing to look Chloe in the eye. "I'm just saying, I don't need to go down that road again."

"Oh, honey..." Chloe leaned across the table and grabbed Faye's hand. "I wasn't suggesting going steady with the guy, just maybe letting yourself have some fun for once."

She knew deep down that Chloe was right. Ever since her relationship with Peter had imploded her life and her heart, she'd thrown herself full-force into teaching and had left little time for anything else. Peter had been her high school sweetheart, and then her college sweetheart, and she'd hoped once they graduated from college, he'd become her husband. They'd been together for so long, that Faye didn't know who she was without Peter. He'd been there for every major life event, birthdays, holidays, graduation... he'd just become this constant, unmovable force in her life that she grew to rely on. So when she'd expected him to propose one night, about a year after they'd graduated college, and he broke up with her instead, her entire being had been turned upside down. Most people thought she should be completely over it by now, and *she was*, mostly. But Faye didn't think there was anything wrong with not wanting to repeat something that like ever again. Sure, she'd put up some walls and made her life completely about work, but she was making a difference in children's lives! She loved her job, and if she was being honest, this was the happiest and most fulfilled she'd felt in a long time.

Well, until Dylan Andersen swooped in with his unreasonable demands and giant ego.

"I don't need fun right now. I need to get through the next few weeks of classes before Christmas."

Chloe put her hands up, as if to surrender. "Okay. Then he's an insufferable prick and you should definitely loathe every second you spend with him."

Faye couldn't help the grin that spread across her face. Chloe was a good friend. Faye thought that if anyone deserved a little fun, it was Chloe. She worked constantly, easily putting in 80 hours per week to run the cafe she built from the ground up. To Chloe, it was a labor of love, but Faye just couldn't fathom the amount of work her friend did each week.

"I could always put in a good word for you, if you'd like," Faye teased.

Chloe shrugged. "Not my type."

"True, he's definitely not *David*," Faye said. David was Chloe's newly hired coffee buyer. Chloe's Coffeehouse would soon be sourcing and roasting its own coffee blends, but with all her time dedicated to running to shop, Chloe had needed to bring in outside help. David Castillo was a seasoned coffee roaster who had experience working with coffee farms in all different areas of South America. He'd been completely on board with Chloe's vision of hand-selected, fair-trade beans that supported small coffee farms in Costa Rica and Colombia, so he was a natural fit. Plus, Chloe had been head over heels for him since day one.

"Shh!" Chloe hissed, swatting at Faye. The smile on Chloe's face, though, betrayed her. *Yep*, Faye thought. *Head over heels.*

"Oh please, everybody already knows. You practically swoon whenever he walks into the room."

"He doesn't know!" Chloe said, and realizing she'd all but confirmed it, bit her bottom lip. "Does he?"

"Only time will tell!" Faye teased, winking at her before they both dissolved into giggles.

"Well, I should be going," Faye said, standing up and sliding on her winter coat. "Thanks for the coffee, and for letting me vent."

"Any time." Chloe stood up and gave her a big hug, then grabbed her by the shoulders. "And don't let anyone, *especially him*, make you feel like you're not the best teacher ever."

"Thanks," Faye said. "I'll try."

She had a feeling it would be easier said than done.

Faye wrapped her coat a little tighter around herself as she headed out of the coffee shop and into the chilly December evening. From the lampposts on Main Street hung giant lit snowflakes and wreathes with big velvet bows. The shops all had string lights illuminating their storefronts, and cheery, Christmas-y displays in the windows. Pine Grove really did embrace the spirit of Christmas, and Faye remembered loving to take walks down Main Street as a child to see all the lights and decorations. When her parents moved south to Florida a few years back, Faye had rekindled the tradition with her grandmother. Since her grandmother's passing this past year... Well, the tradition had become Faye's, and Faye's alone.

A window display of books stacked in the shape of a Christmas tree caught Faye's eye during her walk, stopping her in her tracks. She stood there for a moment, admiring the paper snowflakes that hung around the book tree in the window of the town's one and only bookstore. Brigsby's Bookstore opened its doors in 1912 and had been run by the same family ever since. The bookstore had been one of Faye's favorite places to go since she was a child, in part because of all the history that was preserved in the exposed-brick walls, creaky original oak floors, and 12-foot-tall bookshelves. Melvin Brigsby, the great-grandson of the bookstore's original owner, kept the shop looking much the same as it did when it first opened, and ran it in the same friendly fashion. She'd hadn't been to the town's bookstore in a while, and now that she was here... She figured she could use a few new books for her classroom library. Happy for the excuse to peruse, she stepped inside.

"Well hello there, Miss Parker," Melvin said, standing up from his seat behind the check-out desk when Faye entered the store, the bells above the door chiming as she shut the door behind her. "What brings you in this fine evening?"

"Looking for a few new books for the classroom," Faye said. "The kids love The Magic Treehouse, but I think they're ready for some new adventures."

"Well, I'm sure you know your way to the children's section. You let me know if you need any help now," Melvin said.

"I will Mr. Brigsby, thank you."

The children's section was in the back of the store, with shorter bookshelves so kids could browse, miniature armchairs for reading, and a small stage where story time was sometimes held for the younger children. Faye knew it well, as she often came in to browse for books for her classroom. She headed for the chapter books, looking for anything with magic or animals or sports - all her students' favorites.

She was kneeling down, browsing the very bottom shelf of the chapter books, when she felt as though someone was watching her.

Faye looked up to see a small boy, maybe six or seven years old, looking down at her with a confused smirk on his face. He had curly blond hair and bright blue eyes, and a smudge of dirt across his nose. He looked at the books in Faye's hands, then at Faye, then back to the books and giggled.

"What are you doing?" he asked. Faye smiled at the boy and fanned out the books in her hand.

"Picking out some new books!" Faye said. "Why is that funny?"

"I think..." the boy bent down closer to Faye and whispered, "those are for kids, and you're a grown up."

"Well, they're not for me," Faye said. "They're for my students."

"Are you a teacher?" the boy asked.

"I am," Faye answered.

"I'm gonna have a teacher soon," the boy said. He grinned, and Faye could see he was missing one of his front teeth. The pride he exuded at the prospect of having a teacher confused her, but she played along.

"Well maybe you can help me pick out some books," she said. "My students are about your age. What are your favorites?"

The boy knelt down next to her and scanned the shelves, carefully selecting three books and handing them to her.

"I love these ones," the boy said. "You should get them."

Faye smiled at the boy and added his selections to her pile. "I think I will. Thank you!"

The boy continued browsing, and Faye guessed he had to be in about second grade. She didn't know him, which was odd because of all the second-graders in Pine Grove, Faye taught half of them. She held out her hand. "I'm Faye," she said. "What's your name?"

The boy turned to face her, but before he could answer, a panicked shriek echoed through the small store.

"Ben!"

It was a male's voiced, accompanied by heavy footsteps that were moving closer and closer to them. A pair of black leather work boots and blue jeans appeared in front of them, and Faye's eyes traveled upwards toward the face of the figure looming over them. Faye froze when she realized it was Dylan Andersen.

Dylan scooped up the boy - Ben, as he'd called him, and squeezed him tight. Then, he put Ben down and gave him a stern look. Faye couldn't help feeling foolish about not putting it all together sooner. Ben looked like he was in second grade because he *was*, and Faye didn't know him because they had just moved to town.

"You scared me, buddy. You can't just run off without telling me," Dylan said.

The boy hung his head. "I'm sorry, daddy."

Dylan next turned his disapproving glare to Faye.

"Miss Parker," he said, his surprise at seeing her ringing clear in his voice.

"Her name is Faye," Ben said, and Faye had to stifle a giggle. "And I'm helping her pick out books for her class. I told her all my favorites."

Faye collected her books and stood up. She gave Ben a high-five and thanked him for his recommendations.

"Ben here seems like he's a very accomplished reader," Faye said, looking sheepishly at Dylan. His frown remained.

"He's had a top notch education," he jabbed.

Of course, Faye thought. She closed her eyes and inhaled slowly, reminding herself that violence in front of children was frowned upon. How could she forget the private tutor?

"I should be going," she said, starting to leave.

She'd barely made it out of the children's department when she felt a hand brush across her arm. She turned around, goosebumps exploding across her skin. Dylan had caught up to her, a sheepish look on his face.

"Listen, I'm sorry about what happened in that meeting," he said. Faye could feel the heat climbing in her cheeks and was starting to resent how unsure she felt around him. "I'm sure this situation is not ideal for you, but I really appreciate what you're doing for my son."

"Of course," Faye said. She took a deep breath and decided she could be the bigger person, too. "I'm sorry, too," she said. "I got... worked up at our meeting. You're just trying to do what's best for your child."

Faye had more or less come to terms with the fact that she wasn't going to get around this situation with Dylan Andersen. She'd decided the best thing to do was to accept the status-quo and hope that she stayed out of the small-town rumor mill. Besides, Ben seemed like he might be a model student. It was hard enough to get most of her kids to sit down and read a book, especially when most of them now had iPads or handheld gaming devices. Ben clearly enjoyed reading, which Faye couldn't deny was a breath of fresh air.

"I'll see you on Monday then," Faye said. "For Ben's first day."

"See you Monday," Dylan said. He turned to his son. "Ben, say goodbye."

"Bye!" Ben said. She watched him waving at her as she quickly paid for her books and slipped out of the bookstore. It wasn't until she had disappeared into the busy village street that she finally felt like she could take a deep breath. She only hoped she survived until Monday.

Chapter Five

Dylan watched Faye walk away, a sudden tightness in his chest. He knew moving to Pine Grove would mean experiencing many firsts, both for him and for his son. A single address and a community to belong to were just a few of what Dylan hoped would be welcome changes in both of their lives. Competing professionally, and winning gold at the Olympics especially, had opened Dylan's life up to enough public scrutiny that he desperately wanted a chance for his son to have a normal life. Ben's happiness was his number one priority, which meant that making sure he had a stable home and a normal childhood had to come before anything else. For that reason, Dylan knew he had to ignore the overwhelming urge he had to just reach out and touch Faye whenever she was around. Since he'd first met her, stocking up on sugar at the grocery store, and then going toe-to-toe across her desk, he'd had a hard time focusing on anything besides the way her chestnut brown hair had fallen around her face in silky, spirally curls. He'd wanted to reach out and tuck one behind her ear. It had taken everything he'd had not to. He felt a similar feeling when he looked down and saw her laughing with his son.

Dylan still had his doubts about Ben starting school. He knew Ben would acclimate, kids are resilient and adaptable. Dylan was more worried about himself. He had a good feeling about Faye as Ben's teacher, but the thought of sending Ben off for several hours a day, not having a direct line to his education, made him nervous. Being able to meet with Ben's teacher for a few weeks, and check in on his progress, would go a long way toward putting him at ease with all the changes. Dylan would just have to remember that Faye was Ben's teacher and leave it at that. Crossing that line was a disaster waiting to happen. Besides, Ben had enough questions about his own mother, and the last thing Dylan wanted to do was cause any confusion or hurt feelings for the boy.

"Time to go, Ben," Dylan said, ushering his son toward the exit. Dylan had some cleanup to do around the house before the work crew helping him with renovations arrived the following morning. They would be starting with the kitchen, and although the whole house needed work, the kitchen was the least usable at present. He figured if he could get the kitchen gutted and remodeled, he could give Ben a comfortable, consistent place to eat, do his homework, and bring friends around when he made them.

As they made their way toward the front of the store, they passed an older gentleman behind the customer service desk. His thin gray hair was slicked back on his head, what was left of it trying in vain to conceal a growing bald spot. He smiled at Dylan.

"You must be new here," the man said, extending a hand to both Dylan and Ben. "I'm Melvin Brigsby. This bookstore has been in my family for four generations, so I like to think I know everybody in town. We don't get too many newcomers."

"We just moved here," Dylan said. "I'm Dylan, and this is my son, Ben." Dylan watched his son give the man a tentative wave.

"I see you met Miss Faye Parker," Melvin said. The glint in his eyes returned, and he leaned in closer to Dylan. "I've known Faye since she was a toddler. Well-loved in this town, that girl is."

"Yes," Dylan said, "My son is going to be in her class at the elementary school."

"Lucky boy, then," Melvin said, shooting him a knowing look, as if to make sure Dylan understood just *how* lucky Ben would be.

"So I've been told," Dylan said. "It's going to be a transition for both of us, though." He ruffled his son's hair, and Ben cowered bashfully behind his father.

"Well, you couldn't be in better hands," Melvin said. He leaned in even closer, as if to whisper, despite the store being empty. "Say now,

Faye's a nice girl, but she's been through a lot. It' been a tough year for her. I don't think anyone wants to see her get hurt again."

Again? He wondered what Melvin meant by that, and who had hurt Faye before. He had no intention of hurting anybody, much less his son's teacher. Dylan shook his head. "It's not like that," he said, ignoring the voice in his head that told him it was a lie. "She's going to be Ben's teacher, and that's it."

Melvin nodded, but Dylan could sense he hadn't convinced him. He gave Dylan a warm smile, and shook his hand again.

"Welcome to town, Dylan," he said. He disappeared into a room behind the service counter, leaving Dylan and Ben standing in the shop alone. They turned to leave, when a sudden flash through the glass front door caused them both to jump.

Dylan stood, frozen for a moment, struggling to understand what was happening. Meanwhile, Ben whined and put his hands in front of his face as several more flashes lit up the store. When it finally clicked, anger bubbled up inside of Dylan so quickly, his hands began to shake.

How? How had they found him? Could he really not just enjoy an evening out with his son, without the gossip rags butting in and ruining it for the sake of some lame story? And really, how had they known where he was? He'd been as discreet as he could, not taking any major transit from L.A to New York, buying their fixer upper with cash, so as not to leave a paper trail... and yet they'd *still* managed to track him down?

"Hey!" he yelled, barreling toward the door. He pushed it open, and saw a man dressed in all black holding a fancy-looking camera with a large lens. As Dylan tumbled out into the street, the man pointed the camera at him and clicked, another flash blinding him.

"Knock it off!" Dylan yelled, the sound of Ben whimpering behind him, his son scared at what was happening, causing his blood to boil. "There's no story here, leave us alone!"

The man snapped a few more pictures, the flashes like lightening striking right in front of him. The sound of footsteps thudded behind Dylan, and suddenly Melvin appeared on the sidewalk, shooing the photographer away.

"You get off my property, before I call the authorities! This is trespassing!" he yelled, pulling out a cell phone. The photographer froze for a moment, his camera held in midair, before capping the lens and backing away. Melvin began to dial on his phone, and the photographer took off down the street, disappearing into the dusky evening. They both stood outside the bookshop, watching until he was gone. When the man was completely out of their view, Melvin put his phone back in his pocket, and turned to face Dylan.

Embarrassment washed over Dylan as a tense silence settled between him and Melvin. He knew the media was having a field day with his announcement that he would not be returning to the slopes in next year's Olympics. He'd given interview after interview over the last few months, dispelling rumors about the reason for his exit and confirming that, yes, he really was *done* for good. He'd intentionally left out his plans to move from Los Angeles to the East Coast, for fear of some rogue paparazzi following him for a story. The fact that someone *had* found him, and followed him, and had the gall to take pictures of him and his son without so much as an ounce of discretion, disturbed him beyond belief.

Before he could utter the apology that was begging to escape, Melvin put a hand on his shoulder.

"Are you okay?" he asked.

"Oh, yeah I'm fine," Dylan said, looking to Ben, who was still inside the store. He had his face pressed up against the door, his nose smushed against the glass, watching what was happening on the sidewalk.

"That happen often?" Melvin asked, gesturing into the darkening evening toward the direction the photographer had disappeared. Dylan shook his head.

"Not if I can help it," he muttered. The pair of them went back inside the bookstore, and Ben immediately wrapped himself around Dylan's legs. Ben wasn't exactly a stranger to people wanting to take his father's picture, but such attention wasn't easy to get used to. Pine Grove was supposed to take them away from that life. Dylan felt terrible that clearly, it hadn't made one ounce of difference.

"Well, I don't know much about the paparazzi, being I'm not famous and all, but I do know this - the people of Pine Grove value their privacy, and they look out for one another. You live here now, and that means this town will look out for you, too. We won't stand for nobody trying to disturb your peace," Melvin said. He clapped Dylan on the shoulder and ruffled Ben's hair. "Besides, if word gets out that someone's walking around snapping pictures, ol' Ethel Saperstein might get the wrong idea and think she's got a shot at a cover of Vogue. And trust me, you don't wanna see that."

Dylan chuckled. Melvin's words touched him, especially considering the man hardly knew him. Warmth spread throughout him, and he realized *this*, this was what he'd moved to a place like Pine Grove for. A sense of community. A sense of family.

Dylan spent the following day holed up in the house, working on anything that would keep his mind off of what had happened at the bookstore. He'd enlisted Ben to help him paint some of the walls in the bedroom, showing him how to use the painter's tape to protect the moldings, and how to use the paint roller. His son, of course, had ended up covered in the light gray paint they'd picked for the upstairs bedrooms, but Dylan didn't mind the mess. He wanted this house to be *theirs*, for them to leave their mark on every surface and truly make it their home. So far, they were both settling into small-town Pine Grove life pretty nicely. Once their house was finished, they would be on their way to a normal, quiet life.

Assuming the tabloids left him alone.

In truth, he didn't really care that the gossip magazines were targeting him. He didn't like it, but he'd accepted the invasion of privacy as just part of the life of a well-known athlete. He did not appreciate them dragging his son into it, however. He'd done his best to shield Ben from the paparazzi and influence from the media, and it just burned him that the moment they started to get settled, Ben became a target. What he didn't understand, though, was how they'd managed to find him. He'd been so careful. Then again in Dylan's experience, if the press had a story they wanted to tell, they would find a way to tell it.

His phone vibrated in his pocket and when he pulled it out and looked at the screen, he broke out into a cold sweat. It was a phone call, and it was from his ex-manager, Martin.

Dylan had not heard from his manager since officially announcing his retirement from professional snowboarding. Martin hadn't taken the news very well when Dylan had told him a few days prior, and he hadn't shown up to the press conference Dylan had held from his hospital room. At the time, Martin had felt that the decision to retire was premature, that once Dylan's injuries had healed, he'd be up for competing again. When Dylan remained adamant that he was done, and was going to instead turn his focus to settling down and raising his son, Martin had told him he was throwing away everything they'd worked so hard for. Their professional relationship had ended on a pretty sour note, and they hadn't exactly parted ways as friends.

For that reason, Dylan couldn't imagine why, after making his retirement public and officially leaving the sport, Martin was suddenly calling him up. He had a feeling that, whatever it was, he wasn't about to like it.

"This is Dylan."

"Dylan, buddy, it's Martin! Don't tell me you lost my number already! How've you been?"

Dylan had to pull the phone away from his ear, the booming Long-Island accent on the other end threatening to burst his eardrum. Martin had always been a little larger than life. Some things, Dylan realized, never changed.

"It's just been a while," Dylan said. "What can I do for you?"

"Do for me?" Martin asked, his voice dripping with insincere incredulity. "Nothing, nothing, I was just calling because I saw that article about you. Looks like America hasn't forgotten about you after all."

Dylan tightened his grip on his cell phone, the motivation for Martin's call becoming clearer.

"I think it was just an amateur tabloid hack desperate for a story," Dylan said. "Apparently there isn't anything more interesting going on in the world than some guy renovating a house."

"Makes you miss the spotlight though, don't it?" There was something in his tone, almost a sinister sense of satisfaction that shook Dylan to the core.

There it is, Dylan thought. The real reason for Martin's call. He wondered for a moment if Martin could really go that low, if he could really stoop to that level.

"It was you, wasn't it? You leaked my location to the press?"

It was more of a statement than a question. Dylan already knew the answer. The silence on the other end of the phone only confirmed his suspicions, inciting a burst of white, hot anger to flare up inside of him. He couldn't understand. What kind of person would do such a thing, putting not only Dylan but his child under a microscope for the tabloids? Martin might have been his manager, but he had also been a friend, at least for a while. And for a bit of money and a brief moment of attention, his friend had sold him out.

"I told you, Martin, I'm out," Dylan said. "I'm retired."

"For now," Martin said. "But what happens when you get bored of small-town life? Trust me, in a few months you'll be so stir crazy, you'll be begging me for a way back in. So, why don't we just save ourselves the time and trouble and talk about you coming back and training for the next Winter Olympics?"

"It's not happening," Dylan told him through gritted teeth. "And I'd appreciate it if you'd stop talking to the media about me and my son."

"I'm your manager, it's my job to make you look good to the media," Martin retorted.

"*Were* my manager," Dylan corrected. "Until I retired."

"You should be thanking me," Martin continued, ignoring Dylan. "I was a lot nicer than that stone-cold diva of an ex-girlfriend of yours. Let me tell you, when she found out you moved across the country, for crying out loud? She was *pissed*, I ain't ever seen a woman so pissed in my life."

Dylan froze, his hands clenching into fists at the mention of the woman who'd taken advantage of him, and abandoned their son.

"You talked to Courtney?" Dylan asked, all the pleasantries and professionalism gone from his voice. Martin might want Dylan back as a client, but getting Courtney involved was playing with fire. She'd do anything, no matter who she hurt, to get ahead.

"We'll see," Martin said. "Think about what I said, kid. I'd hate to see you miss your last shot."

"I appreciate the concern, but we're right where we need to be."

Dylan hung up the phone before Martin could get another word in. He worried that he hadn't heard the last of Martin, or seen the last of the paparazzi. Betrayal seared through him, and he realized that now, not even Pine Grove was safe. Nowhere was safe. The imaginary bubble he thought he'd created for him and Ben had burst in an instant, the remnants of what they'd almost had splattered into a thousand tiny fractals.

He couldn't think about snowboarding right now, or Martin, or Courtney. *Especially* not Courtney, not with the way she'd abandoned him and their son without so much as a goodbye. They hadn't heard from her in five years, and it wasn't for lack of trying. Dylan didn't care anymore if she didn't want to be with him, but to completely disappear from Ben's life? How could a mother do that to their own child? He'd only ever tried to get her to have a relationship with their son, but after so many unsuccessful attempts, he'd given up. It was less painful that way, for both him and Ben, than to continue being rejected. What right did she have to be pissed that he'd done what was best for their son? In Dylan's eyes, she'd given that up the moment she'd chosen fame and her modeling career over her son that needed her.

Chapter Six

Something about the early morning, the quiet calm that lie like a blanket over the sleepy town, punctuated by the bright orange and gold sunrise, spoke to Faye. She got her best work done in the early morning hours. For this reason, she chose to spend that time in her classroom, sipping a piping hot cup of coffee with the sun's rays streaming in through tall plated windows, reviewing her lesson plan for the day and preparing any activities she had planned for her students. Then, when her students finally arrived, she could begin the school day with a clear, calm mind and a positive attitude

This morning, however, was not like most mornings.

She'd arrived on a seemingly normal Monday to absolute chaos. Not only had most of the faculty already arrived, despite classes not starting for another hour and a half, but everyone was buzzing around frantically, as if the President of the United States himself might show up at any moment. Faye hurried down the hallway to her classroom, dodging the pointed looks and sympathetic nods each person she passed directed at her. Her chest began to tighten the closer she got to her classroom, and she came to terms with the fact that today, she would have to face Dylan and whatever ridicule from her peers ensued.

Faye had barely reached the door to her classroom when Sylvia Jasper, an art teacher with a notoriously, almost *annoyingly* chipper disposition, gave her an uncharacteristic solemn nod and a pat on the arm.

"Good luck today," Sylvia squeaked, before scurrying off to her own classroom. Faye remained silent, her stomach tensing into a knot. She gave Sylvia a nod and crossed her arms over her chest. Sylvia continued, "I'll admit I'm a little jealous of the eye candy, but I wouldn't wish a parent sitting in on class on my worst enemy."

Faye threw up her hands. "It's insulting!" she said. "Besides, he's insufferable."

"So I've heard," Sylvia agreed. "Although that cute face almost gives him a free pass."

"No, it does not," Faye clenched her teeth so hard her jaw began to hurt. "Wait," she said, spinning on Sylvia and putting her hands on her hips. "What did you hear?"

Sylvia's face went white as a sheet, like she'd been caught.

"Nothing," she said, very unconvincingly. Faye gave her the best stink eye she could muster, given the circumstances, and Sylvia began to backpedal. "*Okay*," she said, "Principal Griffin was talking to Vice Principal Siegel about the meeting last Friday. Apparently, Vice Principal Siegel told Mrs. Smith about all the demands Dylan Andersen made, and she told Mrs. Alfred and Mr. Donovan at band rehearsal, and then somehow Miss McDonald found out, and you know how much of a gossip Angela McDonald is..."

Sylvia trailed off, taking a small step backward. Faye worried her head would shoot off clean from her body, she was so mad.

"Word travels fast," she said through gritted teeth. Sylvia just nodded.

"Small towns."

"Well I'm telling you, I'm not going to stand for any funny business. He can sit quietly and observe, but I won't have him distracting the other children from learning," Faye said.

Sylvia nodded cartoonishly, and Faye knew nobody would believe that. Heck, she didn't even believe it. Suddenly, Sylvia's eyes grew wide and her jaw dropped, and Faye whirled around to see what had caused the reaction.

Vice Principal Annette Siegel strode down the hallway toward them. Except, she didn't look like the Vice Principal.

Faye's jaw hit the floor, and she felt the air leave her lungs in a *whoosh!*

The usually dowdy older woman whom Faye had begun to associate with knitted, patterned sweater vests looked like she'd rolled in from a Vogue photo shoot. Her gray-streaked tresses had been pulled neatly into a bun atop her head, her lashes coated in mascara and her lips tinted a deep berry color. Instead of her usual khaki and sweater combination, Vice Principal Siegel had on a black sheath dress and heels, a string of pearls around her neck. Faye looked from her to Sylvia, whose mouth was agape and whose eyes were bulging out of her head.

"Miss Si...Si...Siegel!" Sylvia stuttered, her hand on her chest as if she might keel over any moment. "You look..."

"Amazing," Faye breathed, hardly able to believe that she was looking at the same woman she'd given an extra-large *Cat Mom* mug for Christmas a few weeks ago.

Annette blushed and swatted them away. "Oh this? This is nothing," she cooed, smoothing her dress down. "Just felt like making more of an effort today, is all."

"Well it's a... it's a lovely change!" Sylvia gushed, but Faye narrowed her eyes at the both of them as a wave of realization crashed over her. *Nothing?* The woman looked as though she'd just stepped off the runway, and it was *nothing?* She pointed an accusing finger toward Vice Principal Siegel.

"This is about Dylan Andersen!" she wheeled around and turned her finger on Sylvia and the Vice Principal disparagingly, causing them both to jump back a little. "I told you this would happen! He's going to be nothing but a distraction to this whole building, let alone my classroom! I'll be lucky if my students pay attention long enough to find their seats when they come in, let alone actually *learn something!*"

"Now, Miss Parker," Vice Principal Siegel said, "I think Mr. Andersen will be a lovely addition to our community. I hope we will all welcome him with open arms, and remember the very *generous* donation he's making to our school."

Faye snorted. "Yes, of course. The *donation*."

Vice Principal Siegel straightened. "And I hope we will be *grateful* that of all the places he could choose to raise his son, he felt highly enough about Pine Grove to settle here."

Sylvia nodded traitorously, and Faye rolled her eyes.

"Yes, we should all be eternally grateful," she muttered. The Vice Principal raised her wrist and checked her watch.

"Miss Parker, shouldn't you be prepping your classroom for the students to arrive? We want everything to look perfect for our guest," she said, derision dripping from every word. Without saying anything, Faye turned on her heel and stalked off toward her classroom, leaving Sylvia and Vice Principal Siegel's chic clone staring after her.

Faye knew she was acting childish. In fact, she knew that her behavior was proving right every concern Dylan had about her experience as a teacher. But Pine Grove, the elementary school... it was her home, and she couldn't help feeling like she was being uprooted by a stranger. Her passion, and work ethic, and her abilities as a teacher were being called into question, and what would happen if, after everything was said and done, he didn't feel she was competent enough? Would he pull his son from her class? Teaching was the only thing she had, and she didn't know what she would do if that was taken away from her. She didn't know who she would be if she couldn't teach.

She busied herself with her usual morning routine, but found it difficult to concentrate on the tasks she normally loved doing. Her stomach did somersaults as the minutes ticked by, and she found herself pacing the empty classroom, her mind consumed with worst-case scenarios. Every now and then, one of the other teachers would poke their head in and say good morning, or wish her good luck, but she could tell by the way they looked around the room that they were just checking to see if *he* had arrived yet. It just added to her anxiety.

At around 7:45, students began to trickle through the hallways, and Faye braced herself. Two students walked into her classroom and waved to her, hanging up their coats and putting their backpacks in their cubbies. To her surprise, the students' mothers followed quickly behind them, their heads together, exchanging hurried whispers and conspicuous giggles. Faye frowned.

Oh no. She ambled over to the chalkboard and wrote the day, month, and year in the top corner in large, swoopy letters, and when she turned around, three more mothers were walking in with their children. As the kids put their things away, the parents all congregated into a back corner of the classroom, whispering loudly. Faye rolled her eyes and took a seat behind her desk, anxiety morphing into annoyance as the gaggle of starstruck mothers continued to grow. Miss McDonald peeked her head in and, seeing the group of women hanging out in the corner, practically galloped up to Faye's desk, a huge smile pasted across her face.

"Are you excited?" she asked in a loud, forced whisper. Angela McDonald taught fifth grade, and though she was in her mid-fifties, she gossiped like a teenage. She dressed like one, too. Today, Angela's hair was in a long, raven-colored braid tossed haphazardly over her shoulder. She wore a pair of jeans with rips in the knees, a black cold-shoulder top with sparkles around the neckline, and knee-high black leather boots. Faye shook her head.

"This is ridiculous," she said. Just as she was about to lament the unfairness of her situation, a collective gasp echoed throughout the classroom, and Dylan appeared in the doorway with his son, Ben.

It was like watching a flock of hungry vultures descend on a dying animal. Dylan barely made it two feet into the door before all of the moms in the corner ambushed him, introducing themselves and fawning over him like groupies. Angela McDonald ran over to join them, which irritated Faye more than the gaggle of mothers did. Faye's eyes immediately went to Ben, who hung back behind his father and stared wide-eyed at the ruckus the moms were causing. She felt a pang of sympathy for the boy, and crossed the room to greet him. His eyes lit up when he saw her.

"Faye!" he exclaimed, and then realizing he'd called her by her first name, correct himself. "Good morning, Miss Parker."

"Good morning, Ben," she said, bending down so she could get closer to eye-level. "Welcome to second grade! Would you like to see your cubby and desk?"

Ben nodded excitedly, and she took his hand and walked him over to the cubbies and coat hangers. She waited patiently while he hung up his jacket and stuffed his backpack into his cubby, then brought him over to his desk. She showed him how he could lift the lid to store his pencils, erasers, and notebooks in there, and then showed him where the classroom pencil sharpener was. Saving what she thought Ben would like best for last, she then showed him the classroom library. He squealed when he saw the books he'd picked out on the shelves.

"You can borrow a book any time you'd like," she told him, "As long as you bring it back when you're finished."

"Wow, thanks Miss Parker!"

Ben ran back to his desk and took his seat, proudly facing the front of the classroom. The flock of women surrounding Dylan had still not dispersed, and the bell was about to ring for classes to begin. Faye could feel herself beginning to get grumpy as she watched the second hand on the clock tick by.

"Excuse me!" she yelled, trying to get the attention of crowd in the back of the room. None of the women paid her any mind, their focus instead completely on Dylan. Several of the women threw their head back in exaggerated cackling, and Faye guessed he must have said something funny or charming. "Excuse me!"

When none of them moved, she picked up the pointer off of the chalkboard ledge and gave it a good whack against the chalkboard. The whole group jumped at once, then turned to face her, startled. Faye smiled victoriously as a blissful silence fell over the classroom.

"We'll be reviewing addition and subtraction of two-and-three-digit numbers today, so unless you need a refresher on that..." Faye gestured toward the open classroom door, "I would like to get class started."

As if on cue, the mothers frowned dramatically and sulked out of the classroom, saying goodbye to Dylan one by one. Faye tapped her foot impatiently as she waited for them to trickle out, the bell that signaled for school to start echoing throughout the room. After a few moments, the only adult besides Faye remaining in the classroom was Dylan. He stood all the way in the back, his hands shoved into his pockets, and his attention fixed directly on her. He eyed her like a predator calculating when to pounce, holding Faye's gaze from across the room. She could barely admit it to herself, but she could understand the mothers. For a moment, everything else fell away, and Faye had to remind herself to breathe. He did look good, all bright-eyed and clean-shaven. She shook herself out of it, and cleared her throat. As infuriating as she found his overconfident male ego, she couldn't deny that there was something... magnetic about him that went beyond pure physical attraction. Maybe it was his celebrity status? She didn't know, and she didn't intend to find out.

"There's an extra chair in the back corner there," she said to Dylan. "You're more than welcome to it."

"Thank you," he said, grabbing the chair from the corner and dragging it back to the middle, so that he was directly in Faye's line of sight.

Great, Faye thought, exhaling sharply. *It's going to be a long day.*

"Class," she said, "we have a new student I would like to introduce to you all." She gestured to Ben, who stood up proudly and smiled. "This is Ben Andersen, and he just moved here to Pine Grove. I know you will all be extra nice to him and make him feel welcome." She addressed Ben, "We're so happy to have you, Ben."

"Hi, Ben," her students all chimed in unison, waving to their new classmate. Her eyes flicked to Dylan, and the adorably proud grin he wore across his face made her heart squeeze.

"Alright, we're going to start by reviewing our homework from last week, so let's all take out our worksheets. Would anyone like to volunteer the answer to the first question?"

FAYE GOT THROUGH MOST of the day without incident, and was surprised that Dylan didn't constantly interject like she thought he would. Ben also impressed her with how engaged he seemed, although he was a little quieter than she might have expected. She'd called on him twice to answer a question, and both times he'd shrunk back into his chair, his face burning with color, so she'd quickly moved on to another student. It was only his first day, though, and she figured a regular classroom environment might feel a little overwhelming to someone who was used to being the only student in the room.

If a celebrity was in the room, the kids didn't know it. Aside from a few more teachers than normal popping into her classroom to "say hi," there weren't many disruptions to class with Dylan being there. In fact, it seemed like the only person truly distracted by Dylan Andersen's presence, was her. She routinely caught herself sneaking a look at him, and a few times, she caught him looking back. Unsurprising, since she was at the front of the classroom teaching, but it didn't change the reaction her body had to his dark eyes bearing into hers. No amount of deep breathing could calm the nerves she'd had since the minute he walked into the room, and no amount of pretending he wasn't there would make the tingling sensation she felt when their eyes met go away. She'd told herself she wouldn't go all starstruck on the man, and yet, here she was.

She turned to her chalkboard and, starting at the top, began writing several vocabulary words in a list on the board until she reached the bottom. "Okay, class," she said, facing her students. "These are our words from last week. Who would like to read the first word, and tell the class what it means?"

A few students' hands flew up, but before she could pick on one to answer, Dylan stood up in the back of the class.

"Excuse me, Miss Parker," he said, "but is 'calm' really a second grade vocabulary word?"

He mouth went dry. Was he really going to question 2nd grade curriculum in the middle of class? She felt her cheeks grow hot as she searched for an appropriate answer to his question.

"Yes, Mr. Andersen," she croaked, realizing she didn't sound even a little bit confident. She cleared her throat. "Are you suggesting it's not?"

"Well, I can say that Ben has been learning more advanced words than these. I'm just wondering if the words you've selected, maybe, aren't challenging enough?"

The other students all turned to look at Ben, who sunk down in his seat as if he was trying to make himself invisible. Faye saw red. She closed her eyes and inhaled a sharp breath, then opened them and turned them like daggers on Dylan.

"Mr. Andersen, let's step outside for a moment."

Without another word, she marched out of the classroom and into the hallway, Dylan close on her heels. She closed the door to the classroom behind them, giving them some privacy in the hallway. He started to speak, but she threw up her finger to shush him. His eyes widened in surprise.

"Mr. Andersen, you want what's best for your son, right?"

He narrowed his eyes at her. "Of course."

"Great. Then in the future, please refrain from singling him out in front of his class like that. I won't tolerate it."

"Excuse me?" he asked, taking a step closer to her. "That's my son we're talking about."

"Yes, and you just embarrassed him in front of all his new classmates. Mr. Andersen - "

"Dylan," he corrected. She rolled her eyes.

"Okay, *Dylan*. Ben is new and trying to make friends. He already has a spotlight on him because *you* are a celebrity. If you want him to have a normal life, and give him the best chance of fitting in and making friends, then you need to let him have the same experience as all the other kids."

"This is because I called you out, right? You're pissed because I think your vocabulary words are too easy?"

"My vocabulary words come directly from the 2nd grade curriculum, so no. Look," she sighed, trying her best to be sympathetic but finding it increasingly difficult. Dylan crossed his arms tightly over his chest, clearly unhappy with her. She straightened and looked him directly in the eye. "Ben is a highly intelligent child. But he's in a brand new environment, and it's going to take some getting used to. Right now, he's not only the new kid in class, but he's the new kid whose famous father is sitting behind him and calling him out in front of all the other students. This transition would be difficult for any child, but you're not making it any easier."

Dylan's eyes fell to the floor, and she prayed she was getting through to him.

"If you have problems with my lessons, that's fine," she said. "You can bring those to me after class, or at one of our weekly meetings. But if you want Ben to thrive, you're going to have to let go a little, and give him some room to grow on his own."

When Dylan lifted his eyes to hers, she saw a whirlwind of emotions flicker through them. He may be a little overbearing, but she couldn't doubt that the man in front of her cared for his son. After a moment, he nodded.

"Okay," he said. "No more interjections, promise."

She exhaled slowly, relief sweeping over her.

"Thank you," she breathed.

"No, thank you," he said. His eyes dropped to the floor again. "Look I uh, I have some errands to run, so I'll head out. I'll be back when school is over to pick Ben up."

"Okay," she nodded. He gave her a weak smile before starting down the hallway, and Faye felt a pang in her chest as she watched him go. She briefly wondered if she'd been too harsh, but quickly shook off the thought. She had been honest. If the truth hurt his pride, there wasn't anything she could do about that.

She took a minute to collect herself in the hallway, then entered her classroom once more. When she got to the front of the classroom, she turned to her students and plastered on her best forced smile.

"Okay, class, where were we?"

Chapter Seven

"So let me get this straight," Chloe said, her gloved hands surrounding an extra-large disposable coffee cup. They were walking through the Colson's Christmas Tree Farm, on a mission to find the best Christmas tree for Faye's house. Over the last few years, this had become their tradition, as well as recruiting some burley bystander to help them cut it down. Faye was only halfway through the week from Hell, so this little outing with her best friend was exactly what she needed. "He just took off after you called him on his crap?"

"Yep." Faye took a sip from her own coffee cup, her eyes scanning the rows of Blue Spruce and Douglas Fir as they walked. "I think I might have hurt his feelings. But you should have seen Ben's face when he called him out in front of the entire class, the poor kid just wanted to disappear!"

"You did the right thing," Chloe said, giving her arm a sympathetic squeeze.

They continued walking, turning down an aisle of dense, dark green Balsam Firs. She inhaled the piney, familiar scent, and sighed happily. The looming holiday season might be stressing her out, but nothing put her more in the holiday spirit than shopping for a Christmas tree. After a few more minutes, she stopped in front of a stout, perfectly conical Balsam Fir tree, and smiled.

"This is the one."

"Alright!" Chloe exclaimed, looking around at the inventory of capable men nearby. "Now we just need someone who can cut this sucker down." She eyed a handful of tall men in jeans and flannels, and winked at Faye. "Excuse me!" Chloe called as she jogged toward them, sending

Faye dissolving into giggles. She could always count on Chloe to keep things interesting.

"You look like you could use some help."

Faye turned at the sound of the deep, familiar voice behind her, and froze. Dylan stood next to Ben, who was bundled from head to toe in a coat, scarf, and knit cap, and pulling a red wagon with a very large Blue Spruce on it. She smiled and said hello to Ben, who proudly told her that he'd cut the tree down himself.

"That's very impressive," she told him, giving Dylan a sheepish look. "I suppose we could use some help."

"We?" Dylan asked, the tone of his question, the lilt of disappointment, causing a stir of butterflies in her stomach.

Faye pointed to Chloe, who was still chatting up the group of flannel-wearing men. "Chloe and I."

"Oh," Dylan said. "Right." He looked down at the ground, then at his son. "Ben, would you like to lend Miss Parker a hand?"

Faye showed Ben which tree, and he excitedly grabbed the little handsaw and got to work. Dylan knelt down beside him and held the tree steady, coaching him on the speed and depth of his cuts. Chloe bounded over, her arms crossed over her chest and one eyebrow cocked.

"I see you found some help," she said, giving Faye a knowing look. They waited as Dylan and Ben finished cutting the tree, and then tossed it onto their wagon next to the Blue Spruce.

"Great job, Ben!" Faye said, giving the boy a high-five. He grabbed the wagon and took off down the aisle toward the baling station. Chloe turned to them.

"I'll keep an eye on him!" she said, flashing Faye a devious smile before taking off after Ben. When they were alone, Faye looked down at her boots and laughed nervously.

"I take it Ben's a fan of Christmas," she said, chastising herself for stating the obvious. Ben was a kid, of course he loved Christmas. Dylan just nodded.

"And what about you?" he asked. They began to slowly walk toward Ben and Chloe, who were in line to send the trees through the tree baler.

"I like it," Faye said. She realized she didn't sound very convincing. "My parents moved to Florida a few years back, they hate the cold. This year, they're on a cruise for Christmas, so I won't really get to see them."

What is wrong with you, she thought. *He doesn't need to know your life story!*

"I definitely get that," Dylan said, shoving his hands in his pockets. "I don't see my family much around the holidays, either. It's always just been Ben and I."

Silence hung between them as they continued walking, until Dylan stopped and turned to face her. She stopped, and waited.

"I need to apologize," he said, taking a step closer. "You were right, I was out of line the other day."

Her surprise rooted her to the ground. She hadn't expected that, especially when she'd been so direct with him.

"No," she said, "I'm sorry. I said some things that weren't very nice."

"You were honest," Dylan said, taking another step toward her. They were close enough now that she could see his breath, feel the warmth radiating off of him. She gulped.

"Yes, but... "

"Thank you," he said. "When you do what I do, people aren't always honest. It can be difficult for them to tell you the truth. You were honest with me, and I didn't react well. For that, I'm sorry."

She didn't know what to say. The way he looked at her so intently, like he needed her forgiveness in this moment, turned her brain into a dark, blank void. He was always so macho, so confident, that this vulnerable side of him took her completely by surprise.

"Apology accepted," she murmured, and he flashed her a brilliant smile that nearly knocked her off of her feet.

"Hey! Are you guys coming or what?" Chloe yelled, jolting Faye back to reality. They both laughed nervously, and Faye looked down at the ground again, hoping the heat in her cheeks wasn't as obvious as it felt.

"I guess we should catch up to them," he said, his eyes still on hers. She nodded, and they made their way to where Chloe and Ben stood with the baled trees. She could feel him watching her, and the intensity of the silence between them caused her stomach to flutter. Could he sense the effect he had on her? *Probably*, she thought wryly. Guys like Dylan had an acute ability to charm women, and unfortunately, it seemed like she was no different, despite her best efforts. While the four of them walked back to their cars, Ben babbled excitedly about the friends he'd made in class so far, what he wanted for Christmas, and how he wanted to decorate their Christmas tree when he and Dylan got it home. They stopped at Faye's car first, and Dylan unloaded her tree into the trunk of her SUV.

"Miss Parker, what kind of lights are you going to put on your tree?" Ben asked, looking at her expectantly.

"I like plain, bright white lights," Faye said, and Ben scrunched up his face.

"We out rainbow lights on," he said. "No offense, but white lights are boring."

Faye shrugged. "You'll have to show me a picture when you're done decorating," she said. Dylan gave her a sheepish look.

"Maybe Miss Parker will come see our tree once it's all decorated?" he said, more like a question, to both Ben and Faye. She thought Dylan looked almost... hopeful.

"Maybe," she breathed, her body flooding with warmth when her response earned her another smile. Chloe cleared her throat, signaling she was ready to get going, and Dylan got the hint.

"Well, we should be going," he said, looking from Chloe to Faye. "I'll see you on Friday for our meeting," he added.

"Yes, I'll see you then."

When Dylan and Ben were out of earshot, Chloe wheeled on her and whacked her on the arm. Faye jumped back, startled.

"What was that for?" she asked, as they climbed into Faye's car and pulled out of the Christmas tree farm.

"You are in so much trouble," Chloe teased. "Tell me everything."

Chapter Eight

When classes let out on Friday afternoon, Faye felt nothing but pure relief. To her surprise, having Dylan in class occasionally wasn't nearly as awful as she'd expected it to be. And it *was* occasionally; other than Ben's first day, he'd only spent a few hours here and there checking in. As much as she hated to admit it, she'd started to look forward to the possibility of seeing him. Ben had adjusted well to the curriculum, too. He was attentive, and hadn't misbehaved once. He was a little quiet, but he was new and that was to be expected. Now that it was Friday, she just had a meeting with Dylan to discuss Ben's first week to look forward to. She had meticulously documented everything about his performance and behavior so she could share it with Dylan, and hoped that he would see there was nothing to worry about. Ben was a good student, and she was sure he would warm up to his new environment eventually. He had made one thing abundantly clear during his first week – Ben *loved* to read. After dismissal, while they waited for Dylan to come by for their meeting, Ben had run right over to the classroom bookcase, yanked a book of the shelf, and sat down to read. Faye sat down at her desk to read through next week's lesson plan, when her cell phone started buzzing at her desk.

There was no phone number, just *Private* emblazoned across the screen.

"Hello?"

"Faye, it's Dylan."

"Dylan?" Faye asked, loud enough that Ben's head whipped up from his book to look at her. She gave the boy a smile and a nod, mouthed that she'd be right back, and slipped out into the hallway. "How did you get this number?"

The slow, deep laugh on the other end of the line caused Faye's toes to curl in her leopard-print flats.

"Small towns," Dylan said, "Everyone knows everything, and everybody talks."

"Figures," Faye said. "Is everything alright?"

"Actually," Dylan said, "I'm in a bit of a situation. I'm doing some renovations at our new house and have some busted plumbing. I've got a plumber on their way here, but if I don't keep pressure on the leak and change out the drip bucket periodically, we'll have a swimming pool for a house."

She gasped. "Oh no."

"Needless to say, I'm going to need to reschedule our meeting. How late do you typically stay at the school?" Dylan asked. "I'm trying to get in contact with Ben's babysitter but not having much luck."

Faye considered for a moment. "Well, I could stay as late as need be," she said, not wanting Ben to be left alone. "Or I could give Ben a ride home."

"I couldn't let you do that," Dylan said. "I wouldn't want to put you out."

"It's okay, really," Faye said. "I don't mind."

She meant it. Ben was a sweet boy, and he'd had a long week at his new school. She could imagine he would want to go home, and not wait around until someone could pick him up.

"Okay, then. Thank you, Faye, I really appreciate it," Dylan said. He gave her their address and directions from the school, and thanked her about a hundred more times before he hung up. Faye helped Ben gather his things, and off they went.

Ten minutes later, Faye pulled into a long gravel driveway lined with overgrown grass and shrubbery. The driveway opened up to a large, dilapidated house built in the Victorian style. The siding was white and chipped, and vines had grown over much of the facade. As soon as Faye put her car in park, Ben hopped out and ran up the rickety porch steps, disappearing into the house. She followed, carefully maneuvering over the creaky wooden boards and through the front door. A voice yelling *I'm back here!* floated to the front of the house, and Faye followed it and Ben's thudding footsteps until she reached the kitchen.

Compared to the outside of the house, the kitchen was in relatively good condition. The floors, Faye would have guessed original hardwood, were in good condition. The cabinets and countertops needed updating, but they weren't falling off their hinges or missing. Faye had noticed the house was in desperate need of updated insulation, as she could feel an icy draft leaking in from the windows, but all in all, it wasn't as bad as she'd expected. Of course, Dylan, whose torso was mostly engulfed by the cabinet under the sink, legs sticking out, probably felt differently.

"What happened here?" Faye asked. Dylan slid out from under the sink, one hand still holding a pipe together, and Faye felt like the wind had been knocked out of her.

The faucet was running, and the countertop and floors were wet. Dylan wore blue jeans, and a white t-shirt that had clearly been a victim at some point of the plumbing incident. Fabric clung to his abdomen, and Faye saw ripples that suggested muscles it was better she didn't think about right now.

"Pipes must have frozen at some point," Dylan said. He gestured to the one he was holding together. "I turned the faucet on and the pipe burst. Then the faucet froze. I can't turn it off."

Faye had to stifle a giggle. Old houses usually came with a few problems. In the case of Dylan's old house, it seemed he had his work cut out for him.

"Sounds like a mess," Faye said.

"I have a plumber on the way, but until they get here I'm a bit stuck. I've been under this sink for half an hour."

The sound of loud, thudding footsteps shook the old house. A distressed *Daddy!* echoed throughout the house. More footsteps thundered above them, followed by another cry for Dylan.

"Daddy I can't find Jack!"

Ben sounded upset, and Dylan looked conflicted, as if he didn't know what to do. His hand held a plastic shopping bag tight around the pipe, preventing a majority of the leak but tying him to the kitchen sink.

"Who's Jack?" Faye asked. Dylan sighed.

"Jack is Ben's teddy bear," Dylan explained. "It's his favorite toy."

"Ah."

"Ben's room isn't unpacked yet, so Jack is probably still tucked in a box somewhere," Dylan said.

"*Daddy!*" Ben yelled again. This time, he sounded as though he was crying.

"Just a second, buddy!" Dylan yelled back. "Daddy's a little busy right now!"

Ben's distraught sniffles broke Faye's heart, and she could tell it pained Dylan to not be able to do anything.

"Why don't I take over," Faye offered, "so you can help Ben find Jack."

"The plumber will be here in a few minutes, Ben will be okay until then," Dylan said. Ben's crying became louder, and Dylan checked the watch on his free arm.

"Really," Faye said. "I can handle it for a few minutes. Do you have any tape?"

"Tape is still packed," Dylan said.

"Alright, I can just hold it then."

Faye crouched down next to him, trying hard not to react to being so close. He carefully slid out a bit from under the sink, one hand still on the burst pipe, and grabbed Faye's hand with his other one. She maneuvered under the sink while he guided her hand, inhaling an intoxicating blend of citrus and cedar as she settled just inches from him. Her hand replaced his, holding the tightly wrapped plastic in place around the broken pipe.

"Thank you," he said. She was close enough that she could see the bags under his eyes and the stubble on his jaw. He looked tired. He climbed out from under the cabinet. "I'll be right back."

Dylan disappeared out of Faye's line of sight, and she finally felt like she could breathe again. She felt sorry for Dylan that renovations and problems with the house were preventing them from settling in. Moving was stressful, for children especially, and her heart ached for Ben, who so obviously wasn't comfortable yet. She had lived in Pine Grove all her life, and besides college, hadn't really known anything else. She couldn't imagine suddenly being uprooted and trying to make an unfamiliar place her home, especially at that age. It was probably taking a toll on the both of them.

Her pulse had just begun to return to normal, when she caught movement out of the corner of her eye. Slowly, and taking care not to shift her grip on the pipe, Faye lifted her eyes toward the top of the cabinet. It was dark under there, and Faye had to squint as she searched for the source of the movement. When she didn't see anything, she wondered if she had just imagined it. She was trying to reassure herself of that when it happened. Her worst nightmare.

A spider, all spindly-legged and bulbous-bodied, began to drop from a web right above her head.

The scream, like something out of a horror movie, caused the hairs on the back of Dylan's neck to stand up. He set a much happier Ben and his bear down on the floor and tore out of Ben's bedroom. He raced down the staircase, skipping every other step, a million worst-case-scenarios running through his mind. When he made it to the kitchen, his chest heaving and his hands reaching for his cell phone in case he would need to call 911, he couldn't believe what he saw.

A drenched Faye sat huddled in a ball on the floor, her hair all stuck around her face, surrounded by a shallow pool of water leaking from under the sink. Her eyes were wide, and she was trembling, as if she'd just seen a ghost, or witnessed a murder. Dylan grabbed the role of duct tape he'd found and stuck in his back pocket and dove under the sink, wrapping the plastic bag around the crack in the pipe and taping it securely in place. He replaced the drip bucket, and then went to Faye.

"Faye, are you alright? What happened?" he asked, moving sopping tendrils of hair out of her eyes and away from her nose. She swallowed hard and looked up at him with those big hazel eyes, terrified.

"Sp...sp...sp...spider," she murmured, then winced, as if recalling a particularly harrowing memory. Dylan fought back the laughter bubbling up inside of him.

"A spider?" he asked. She winced again and swallowed hard.

"A *big* spider."

Faye looked around at the mess in the kitchen, her eyes growing even wider. Dylan helped her up.

"I'm so sorry," Faye said. "There was just a *huge* spider, and it started coming toward my face and I didn't know what to do. I *hate* spiders."

"Are you okay?" Dylan asked. Faye whipped her head around, searching for anything to sop up the water on the kitchen floor with.

"I'll clean all this up, I'm so sorry," she said. She spotted a roll of paper towels on the card table in the dining area and lunged for them. She began unrolling. "You may need to get inside the cabinet though. In case there are more spiders."

"*Faye*," Dylan said, grabbing hold of the paper towel roll and placing it on the counter. He bent down so he was face-to-face with her. "Are you okay?"

Faye sucked in a deep breath and nodded.

"I'm fine. A little embarrassed, but fine."

Faye took the wad of paper towels in her hand and started to soak up the water on the floor. Dylan unraveled a few feet of paper towels himself and helped her. They worked until the floor was mostly dry, and the evidence of Faye's mishap was nothing more than a pile of paper towels in the garbage.

"Did Ben find his bear?" she asked, and Dylan was grateful for the break in the awkward feeling that had settled over their silence.

"Yes," Dylan said, "thank God. It would have been a disaster if Jack had been really lost."

"That's sweet he's so attached. Did you give it to him when he was a baby?" Faye asked. Dylan's face darkened, and he shook his head.

"His mother gave that to him, before she decided being a wife or a mom wasn't something she wanted," Dylan said. His matter of fact tone confused Faye. She couldn't tell if he was angry, or sad, or disappointed. She couldn't tell if he was all of those things, or none of them. "It's the only thing Ben really has of her."

"I see," Faye said. "I'm so sorry."

"Oh, don't be," he said. "It wouldn't have worked out. It's been confusing for Ben, though. And he never goes anywhere without that bear."

She nodded, and Dylan wondered if he'd divulged too much. She probably didn't want to hear about his past relationship problems, but for some reason, he felt like all his walls came down around her. Why was that? Why did he feel like he could open up to this woman who was practically a stranger? *She's honest*, he thought. *Real.* He wasn't used to that. He noticed her wrap her arms a little tighter around herself as she shivered involuntarily.

"You must be freezing," he said. "Let me get you some dry clothes, you can't go out in this weather soaking wet like that."

Faye started to protest but couldn't bring herself to follow through. She really was freezing. Dylan didn't wait around for her, either. He darted up the stairs, returning a few moments later with an oversized pair of sweatpants and a long-sleeved t-shirt emblazoned with the Olympic rings and "Sochi 2014."

"Put these on," Dylan said. There was a knock on the door sighed, relief washing over him. "The plumbers. Finally." He started toward the door, and then turned back around. "The bathroom is just around the corner, you can get changed in there."

Faye did as she was told, grateful to change into something warm and dry. She could hear Dylan letting the plumbers in, and showing them to the kitchen. Faye hoped they'd be able to fix it right away. Not being able to use running water certainly wouldn't help Ben settle in. She pulled the shirt over her head and laughed when she saw herself in the mirror. She practically drowned in the dark fabric, but the last time she'd worn a man's shirt like that was in college, so she kind of liked the way it looked and felt.

She folder her wet clothes and padded back toward the kitchen, where she passed the gorgeous Blue Spruce, all decked with lights and garland, that they'd cut down a few days earlier. A smile tugged at the corner of her lips at the memory of that evening. After their moment, she'd noticed a marked shift in his attitude toward her that she couldn't quite explain. It was as though a switch had flipped. He'd stopped sitting in on classes, and instead spent a few minutes around at drop off in the morning and pick up in the afternoon to chat with Faye about Ben's progression. He'd even brought her a coffee one afternoon from Chloe's, which had spurned several nosey texts from Chloe later that day wanting to know why Pine Grove's resident celebrity was asking around for Faye's coffee order.

When she made it to the kitchen, she saw the plumbers were working away on the sink and Dylan was supervising. He looked up when she entered the room and grinned, his eyes crinkling in a way that made legs go a little wobbly.

"Thanks for the dry clothes," Faye said, her eyes drifting to the floor. That was the only place the view didn't seem to make her pulse flutter. She willed the silly thoughts to go away. Going all starstruck at the man was the last thing she needed to happen.

"No problem at all," Dylan said. They stood there for a beat, neither saying a word, the silence humming around them like electricity.

"I should be going," Faye said.

"Oh, of course," Dylan said. "Thank you for bringing Ben home today, and for, well... sorry about the pipe."

"It's okay." Faye didn't know why she was blushing, but she could feel her cheeks getting hot. "Goodbye," she said, starting toward the door. Dylan caught up with her.

"Are you free tomorrow morning?" Dylan asked, his amber eyes piercing. "Better yet, how do you feel about breakfast?"

Faye just blinked at him, not sure she could actually be hearing what she thought she was hearing. Breakfast? With Dylan? Faye felt about breakfast the way most people felt about church – it was a sacred practice to be respected and engaged in frequently, especially on the weekends. Even still, the idea of a breakfast date with Dylan felt oddly intimate.

Date.

The word ricocheted around her brain like a pinball. She absolutely could not go on a date with Dylan Andersen.

"Oh, I'm not sure that's a good idea..." Faye couldn't look him in the eye. A part of her, bigger than she liked to admit, wanted to yell *I'm free!,* but she knew how completely inappropriate it would be given that she was his son's teacher. She looked for the words to tell him exactly that, when his eyes became saucers and he started to shake his head.

"I meant, to discuss Ben's first week," he said. "I know it's the weekend, but I would really like to discuss it, and breakfast can be on me since I put you out so much today."

Embarrassment stung like a cattle prod, white hot and sharp. Faye wished she could condense herself into an infinitely tiny speck and float away. What on earth was wrong with her that she would assume Dy-

Ian was asking her out on a date? She tried to recall if she'd bumped her head during her run in with the spider. It was the only sane explanation.

"Right," she said, "of course." Of course he would still want to have the meeting, that had been the deal, after all. "Yes, I can be available tomorrow morning."

"Great, let's plan on 10:30. I'll text you the details," Dylan said. He waved and went back into the kitchen to check on the plumbing crew, and just like that, Faye was alone in his foyer, wearing his sweatpants and t-shirt, feeling like a complete idiot.

Hopefully, she could find her pride before tomorrow morning.

Chapter Nine

Faye stood outside Chloe's Coffeehouse, a mixture of anticipation and dread churning in her stomach. She had brought Dylan's clothes, washed, and neatly folded, and her notes from the prior week. They were meeting for breakfast and coffee, and in an effort to highlight that this was most certainly *not* a date, Faye had chosen to wear jeans and an innocuous, shapeless black sweater. She'd put her hair up in a ponytail and used minimal make up, hoping the more casual this meeting felt, the less nervous she'd be. Meeting in her classroom would have been one thing; there, Faye was in her element. As she stood outside of the little café, shivering despite her large winter coat, a million different anxious thoughts crept into her brain.

What if a parent of one of her students saw them together? Would they assume she and Dylan were discussing Ben? Or would they assume something was going on between the two of them? She hadn't wanted to appear too dressed up, hoping to dispel any notion that their meeting was more than just that, but she found herself now second guessing her appearance, too. Did she look too casual? Would showing up to breakfast like she'd just rolled out of bed suggest that they were a little *too* comfortable with one another?

Faye saw only losing options.

She took a deep breath and propelled herself through the door, scanning the small dining room for Dylan. She caught Chloe's eye first, who smiled wide when she saw her and waved, her other arm pouring a cup of coffee for a customer in line at the counter. Faye spotted Dylan at a table in the corner, a large cup of coffee in front of him, and made a determined beeline toward him. As she did, she watched Chloe's smile morph into a silent gasp, the look on her face assuring Faye that she would press for details later.

Dylan looked up when he saw her coming and smiled. He was going to have to stop doing that if Faye planned to keep her sanity at all. She could see he hadn't shaved, and that dark circles rimmed his eyes, and she wondered if all the unpacking and renovations were catching up to him. As she sat down, Chloe brought over a ceramic mug and set it down in front of her. She narrowed her eyes at Faye mouthing "*later*", and then hurried off back to the espresso machines.

"I hope the kitchen sink is fully operational this morning," Faye said. She took a sip from her cup and sighed. If an award for making the most perfect foamy cappuccino existed, Faye thought Chloe should get it.

"It took most of the evening, but we now have a fully functioning kitchen."

"That's great news," Faye said. "Where's Ben today?"

"He's with his babysitter," Dylan said. "Figured he might feel a little odd sitting here while we talked about him."

"Well I only have good things to say," Faye said. She opened the planner she'd brought with her and flipped to the prior week. Each week had a section for note-taking, and she used it to keep track of any accomplishments or setbacks her students had that particular week. She showed it to Dylan, explaining that there were two columns, each with a roster of her students. In the left column, she tracked any time each a student did something worthy of praise, such as meeting a goal, asking a great question, or showing leadership. In the right column, she tracked when a student did something that was disruptive or poor behavior, such as passing notes, talking during quiet time, or interrupting other students. It wasn't a perfect system, but by tracking the good with the bad, she made sure to praise her students when they deserved it, and not just correct their bad behavior.

"That's very thorough," Dylan said. "And Ben had a good week?"

"He was very attentive," Faye said. "He didn't misbehave, he completed his homework, and I can tell he loves to read."

"Sometimes I think I'll go broke buying him new books, he reads them so fast," Dylan said. Faye recalled running into them at the bookstore, and Ben picking out several favorites.

"He was a little shy and quiet, but that's totally normal for a child in a new environment like that," Faye added. "He's making friends, so I'm sure the shyness will wear off with time."

"I think that's what I'm most worried about," Dylan said. "He's so quiet, and very shy. I'm worried he'll have a hard time making friends, or that he'll get picked on and won't be able to stand up for himself."

"I can assure you, we keep a very close eye on bullying," Faye said. "But socially, he seems to be doing just fine/"

"I'm sure you do, but it can still happen. Plus, being my kid... that could alienate him from the other students."

Faye was confused. Alienate him? Being the son of a celebrity, she envisioned everyone would want to be Ben's friend. "If anything, I'd think that would make him more popular," she said. "The whole town's been talking about you moving here for months."

"Maybe," Dylan said. "Or they could take advantage of him, and Ben will end up being the one getting hurt."

"I don't think you're giving the people of Pine Grove enough credit," Faye said. "They're good people. *We're* good people."

"I'll guess we'll find out," Dylan said.

Faye sat quietly, drinking her cappuccino, and contemplating everything Dylan had just laid in front of her. Clearly, he'd been hurt before and was trying to avoid the same happening to his son. Faye couldn't help but wonder if Ben's mother was the source of all that pain. Under what circumstances had she left Dylan? And what could possibly have driven her to leave her son, who wanted and needed a mother in his life? The thought was baffling to Faye. She'd taught children from broken homes or complicated family situations, and she'd seen how it could affect their self-esteem, ability to make friends, and performance in school. She wondered if Ben was going through that right now.

"It must be really hard raising Ben on your own," Faye murmured. She hadn't meant to say it out loud, and she wished she'd kept it to herself. But, she *had* said it, so now she'd have to deal with whatever came next. She lifted her eyes to meet his and braced herself. The way Dylan's eyes had darkened told her everything she needed to know.

"I'm not talking about me, here, if that's what you're thinking," he said. His sudden defensiveness was like a punch to the gut.

"Of course not," Faye said. "We're talking about Ben. I'm sorry, I didn't mean to pry."

Dylan softened, and Faye felt relief wash over her. They both took a sip of their coffee, and Dylan shook his head.

"I'm sorry, Ben's mother is just a bit of a sore subject. It's been an adjustment for the both of us, but I think we're finally getting a good place."

"I can't imagine," Faye said, instinctively reaching her hand out to touch his arm. "If there's anything I can do. . ." She saw the heat that flared in Dylan's eyes, and pulled her hand back. Her mouth had suddenly gone dry. What had possessed her to do a thing like that? "If there's anything I can do for Ben, please let me know."

"Of course," Dylan said, taking another sip of his coffee when a bright flash momentarily blinded them. "What the hell?"

Faye's head whipped around, and she spotted a man by the door to the cafe. A large, expensive looking camera hung from a thick leather strap around his neck. It took a moment for her to understand what was happening.

"Is he taking pictures of you?" she asked Dylan. He nodded, although it didn't look like he quite believed it was happening, either. "Does this happen often!?"

The humming of chatter in the cafe had faded, and all heads were turned toward Dylan. Faye shrank in her chair, the sudden attention making her uncomfortable.

"Dylan, is it true you're out of the game for good? No more Olympics?" the photographer asked. He snapped another photo, and Dylan remained paralyzed in the bright flash. "What brought you to this tiny town?" the photographer continued. Another bright flash. "How is your son taking the move?"

His son.

Dylan snapped to attention. How had they found him? He was used to such assaults when he was training or during a competition. But he'd already made a statement to the press that he was retiring. He'd already removed himself from the competition circuit. What could they possibly be trying to dig up? He got up from his seat.

"I have no comment, please leave me alone."

The photographer turned his camera to Faye. Another bright flash filled be room.

"Is this you're new girlfriend?" The photographer asked. "How does your son feel about having a new mother-figure in his life?"

"I said, I have no comment," Dylan said again.

"What's going on here?"

Chloe appeared next to Dylan, a broom in her hand. He wondered if she planned to use it for more than sweeping, if necessary. The photographer ignored her, and instead continued to press Dylan for answers. Chloe stepped in front of Dylan, blocking the photographer's view.

"You need to leave, now," she said. "Or I'll have the sheriff come drag your butt out."

"Chill, lady, I'm not breaking any laws," the photographer said. Chloe closed the space between them and gripped her broom tighter.

"But you are disrupting my place of business. Now beat it!"

The photographer put a lid on his camera lens and hightailed it for the door, glaring at Dylan in a way that Dylan knew this wasn't over, he'd be back for more. He looked at Faye, who was wide-eyed and red-faced across from him. She wouldn't make eye contact with him, instead just staring straight ahead at the wall behind him. The air in the cafe was silent and still.

"I'm so sorry about that, "Dylan said. "I have no idea how they found me. Or why they wanted to."

"I should go," Faye said, standing up and slipping on her coat. "Thank you for the coffee."

Dylan watched her head for the door, not far behind the photographer, and stood up to follow her.

"Faye!" he yelled, chasing after her. "Wait up!"

She slowed and looked back at him, but did not stop walking. He caught up with her on the sidewalk outside the cafe.

"Hey what about breakfast?" he asked. The question felt silly the minute it left his mouth, but he *had* promised her breakfast. After what Faye had just been through, he couldn't help feeling like he needed to make it up to her somehow.

"It's okay, really," Faye said, turning around to give Dylan a weak smile. "I'll see you in class."

She disappeared into the sea of Saturday morning Main Street shoppers, and Dylan let her go. Between the burst pipe and the paparazzi, he'd burdened Faye enough. Even though he was used to dealing with tabloids and the media, he still hated the paparazzi and their relentless pursuit of a juicy story that didn't exist. The thought brought to mind his ex-girlfriend and mother of his child, Courtney, and he couldn't help but laugh.

Contrary to Dylan's feelings, Courtney had always loved the attention. Craved it. He'd met her during a winter sportswear photoshoot where Dylan was the featured celebrity athlete. Courtney had been a budding model at the time, and had chatted and flirted with him the entire shoot. Dylan asked her to dinner after the shoot, they'd hit it off, and started dating shortly after. He remembered feeling like he'd finally hit it big, sitting across from her at some fancy restaurant he couldn't remember the name of now. He'd just landed some big-name sponsors, was training for his second go at an Olympic gold medal, and now, he was dating model. He felt like a rockstar.

Courtney had adjusted quickly to life as a famous athlete's significant other. While Dylan would wear baseball caps and sunglasses wherever he went to conceal his identity, ducking from reporters and cameras, she would seek them out. She would wave when the paparazzi took pictures and answer questions from reporters, and Dylan started to realize Courtney liked the constant invasion of privacy. In the beginning of their relationship, their differing views on media involvement in their lives was the biggest thing they fought about. Until, of course, Courtney got pregnant.

Dylan had been ecstatic when she broke the news. 23 years old at the time, he'd been young and naïve and enamored with the thought of starting a family. Courtney hadn't been so thrilled. Her modeling career was just picking up steam, and an unplanned pregnancy might as well have been her worst nightmare. They'd fought over the past, present, and future. Over who made the decision to forgo contraception, over what they were going to do in the moment, and over what they would do when the baby was born. Courtney was adamant that she wanted to give the baby up for adoption, and that the two of them weren't ready for a child. As much as it killed Dylan on the inside to think about giving his child up, he respected Courtney's feelings. Her perspective shifted dramatically, however, when she'd started to show.

The media ate it up. Courtney, in turn, ate up the attention. The sudden positivity from Courtney had made Dylan hopeful again that they could still have a family, and for the remainder of her pregnancy, they were truly, genuinely happy. After Ben was born, the excitement wore off for Courtney almost instantaneously. The reality of parenting a child set in, and the media and paparazzi became much less interested in the model-turned-mother, which drove Courtney crazy. Dylan, admittedly, hadn't been around as much as he should have been. He was training longer and harder as the Olympics drew closer, and Courtney took on the responsibility of caring for their infant. The first chance she got to jump ship, to run headlong back into the modeling world and leave Dylan and the responsibility of being a parent behind, she took it. She hadn't looked back.

Dylan shook the memory and headed to Iris' house to pick up Ben. He pushed the thoughts about Courtney and the media, and even Faye, from his mind. It would do him no good to dwell on the things he couldn't change or control. He needed to remember to leave the past in the past, and keep moving toward the future.

Chapter Ten

Faye felt like one of her second-graders standing outside of Principal Griffin's office. She looked down at her brown leather booties and stockinged legs, digging her toe into the linoleum floor and twisting it around, like a guilty child who'd just been scolded. The office door was closed, and she could hear the muffled voice of her boss behind it, his tone even and stern. The churning in her stomach only intensified.

Typically, if Bob had a question or a concern, he would shoot her an email or stop by her classroom. He'd never before paged her over the loudspeaker like a student in trouble. She sensed the impromptu meeting had something to do with the tabloid article making the rounds about her and Dylan, and she wasn't ready to face that yet. She knew she would have to, of course. All of the gossip rags were calling her *Dylan's Newest Fling*. It had been a full week since their run-in with the photographer, and she still felt scared to go out of the house. By now, everyone had seen it, apparently even her boss.

The door swung open, and two young boys shuffled out with their heads hung low. Faye sucked in a deep breath and waited until she heard Bob's somber voice summoning her.

"You may enter, Miss Parker."

Faye trudged sheepishly into the office, trying to summon the same bravado she'd managed the last time she'd met with Bob to discuss Dylan Andersen. Of course, she hadn't been in the center of a salacious rumor last time. She steadied her breathing and lifted her gaze to meet her boss's, the disapproving look on his face cutting through her life a knife.

"Before you say anything," Faye said, unable to control the words from spilling forth. "You have to believe me that none of it is true. There is nothing going on between Dylan Andersen and I."

"Miss Parker..." Bob started to speak, but Faye steamrolled him.

"We were discussing Ben when that photographer found us," Faye continued, barely skipping a beat. "I know what it looked like, but I swear, it was purely professional."

"Miss Parker..."

"Really, there is absolutely nothing going on. I would never compromise my professionalism just because some famous athlete -"

"Faye," Bob said, his voice rising a few decibels. This caught Faye's attention, causing the verbal freight train barreling from her mouth to come to an abrupt halt. Bob tilted his head and gave her a weak, if sympathetic smile. "I know."

"Know what?" Faye asked, struggling to rein in her thoughts and catch up to the conversation.

"I know that article is nothing more than a horrible piece of gossip."

"Oh." Relief washed over her, and for a moment Faye was speechless. Then, as if a switch had been flipped, confusion replaced the momentary peace of mind. "If that's true, then why did you call me down here?"

"Well, I wanted to see how you were holding up," Bob said. "I can't imagine having a camera thrust in your face and rumors spread about you like that is a pleasant experience, and I wanted to let you know that I'm here if you need anything from me."

Faye bit back the tears welling up in her eyes, swallowing the lump that had formed in her throat. Her boss's small display of support had surprised her, and the sentiment meant more to her than she expected. She let a small sniffle escape, and then, the floodgates opened.

Bob got up from his desk and walked around to her, handing her a box of tissues with one hand, and gesturing for her to sit with the other. Faye took a seat, blowing her nose into a tissue.

"Thanks," she murmured, working hard to keep her voice from wavering. She felt pathetic, but the reality of not having anyone to turn to was starting to catch up to her. She could call her parents, but they'd probably be furious at the possibility of a scandal and give her some self-righteous sermon about her choices and lying in the bed she'd made. Her father never hesitated to lay blame squarely on her, especially when his precious political reputation could be at stake.

"You should also know that your weekly meetings with Ben's father will no longer be necessary," Bob added.

There it was. The real reason for this summons. Faye wiped her nose with her tissue and gave a quick swipe under her eyes with her thumbs. She should feel happy at the news, but she didn't. Instead, she felt as though she'd failed. If she hadn't met with Dylan on Saturday, if she hadn't been so caught up in the butterflies she felt whenever he so much as looked at her, that photographer wouldn't have had a story to tell. At least, not one involving Faye.

"With all due respect, that won't be necessary," Faye quipped. "I agreed to these meetings and I want to make good on my word. You don't need to cancel them just because I got myself into a pickle."

"Oh, that's not why they won't be necessary," Bob said. "Mr. Andersen decided to cancel them. He said he feels comfortable with you as Ben's teacher and doesn't think he needs them."

His words were like a punch to the gut. Canceling had been Dylan's idea? After that photographer had plastered their faces together and suggested a romantic attachment, she wondered if Dylan just didn't want to be associated with her in that way. She supposed she wouldn't blame him. He had a whole life she didn't know anything about. Maybe he even had a girlfriend. Had that article complicated other areas of his life, too? Faye suddenly felt selfish for thinking she'd been the only victim.

Her shoulders sagged. Was the electricity she'd felt between them just in her imagination? Were the goosebumps that exploded across her skin whenever he was close to her just a one-sided daydream? She felt foolish.

"I thought you'd be happier," Bob said. "You weren't an advocate for these meetings at the start."

Faye forced her chin up. She would not be disappointed. In fact, she would be grateful. She'd let her feelings get in the way of her better judgment, and had become exactly the type of person she was trying to avoid - a starstruck, lovesick groupie. Without their meetings, she would get a much needed detox from Dylan Andersen.

"I suppose I'm just..." she hesitated, searching for the right word. "Surprised."

"Are you sure it's not something else?"

Well, she thought wryly. *I guess I'm more transparent than I thought.* She fidgeted in her seat. "I'm sure."

"Well, I bet this whole mess will all blow over soon. Don't forget, let me know if you need anything in the meantime."

"Thanks, I will. And Bob..." Faye said, dreading to say what was on the tip of her tongue, but knowing she had to. It was the only right thing to do, given the circumstances. "If you think someone else should man the table at the Holiday Festival, I understand."

It pained her to say it, but she knew it was the only thing to do. The town's annual Holiday Festival had been a staple in Faye's life since before she could remember, and was a Pine Grove tradition. A few years ago, Faye had suggested setting up a table at the Festival for the elementary school to accept donated school supplies as a way to make sure no student ever went without basic school necessities, like pencils, and erasers, and notebooks. The first year they put up the table, the town donated so many school supplies, there was enough to supply all the students in the elementary and middle schools for a full year. The second year, no student in the high school found themselves lacking for a pencil or fresh notebook, either. The third, there were so many school supplies donated that the town began turning to neighboring school districts to see if they could use any extra supplies. For its fourth year, Faye was hoping to break a record with her little donation table. It was too bad she wouldn't get to be a part of it this year.

She turned to leave, desperate to be away from her boss's pitying gaze. Before she could reach the door, Bob called her back.

"Faye, don't be silly," he said. She stopped, taking in a deep breath, and swiping the tears that had started to trickle down her cheek away before turning around. "There is no donation table at the Festival without you, you know that. That muckraking garbage of an article doesn't change that."

"But my face has been smeared all over the internet. That can't be good publicity for the Festival, especially since I'm sure there will be plenty of media outlets there for Dylan already," she said.

Bob looked as though a light bulb had just gone off in his brain. He shot up from his chair, his eyes alight and a smile from ear to ear, and Faye instinctively took a step back. He put one hand on his hip while the other rubbed his shiny, mostly-bald head.

"Faye," he murmured, his voice taking on a dream-like quality. "You're a genius!"

She frowned.

"I am?"

"Yes!" Bob exclaimed. "We'll use the media coverage to draw more attention to the Festival, and to the school supply donations. It's completely brilliant!"

"It is?"

"Yes. In fact. . ." He gave her a conspiratorial look. "You and Dylan should work the donations table *together*."

"*What?*"

Faye dug her nails into her arm just to make sure she wasn't dreaming or hallucinating. The twinge of pain she felt told her that, unfortunately, she had heard her boss just fine. Her name and face had just been splashed all over the internet next to Dylan Andersen's, and he wanted her to intentionally use that to get more publicity? He spun around and walked back to his desk, and began tapping frantically on his keyboard. Faye lurched behind him and peered over his shoulder, her eyes growing wide as she saw him begin an email addressed to none other than Dylan himself, with the Superintendent cc'd.

"Can't we talk about this first?" Faye asked, not wanting to seem insubordinate, but also desperately wanting to shove her boss's computer right off his desk at watch it combust into a pile of ashes.

"What's there to talk about?" Bob asked, still grinning from ear to ear, and clearly pleased with himself. "The publicity from the Festival will completely overshadow this little smear campaign, and plus, it will draw more attention to a great cause! We'll have our best donation year yet!"

She could see his point, but the part of her brain that had resigned itself to being free of Dylan protested emphatically. She was supposed to be detoxing, for crying out loud!

He hit 'send,' and she closed her eyes as the only chance she had of things getting back to normal disappeared into cyberspace.

"Done!" Bob exclaimed. "I'll let you know what he says. I'm sure he'll be all for it!"

Great, she thought. *I can't wait.*

DYLAN CLOSED OUT OF his email and stuffed his phone into his pocket, exhaling sharply. Bob Griffin's words when they'd spoken on the phone earlier replayed in his head like a broken record.

I'll give Faye the news.

He supposed Faye would be delighted to know that she would no longer need to uphold her commitment to weekly meetings with him. Dylan knew they truly weren't necessary. It was clear to him that Faye was more than competent, and Ben enjoyed having her for a teacher.

The fear of letting go that had once seemed insurmountable had disappeared the moment he'd seen Faye sitting with his son on the floor of Brigsby's, surrounded by stacks of children's books. As much as he should have been satisfied that he could check Ben's education off the list of things he needed to worry about, he couldn't shake the feeling of disappointment eating at him. Now, though, was no time to be selfish. Seeing Faye get hassled by that slimy photographer had made him realize that the spotlight that constantly followed him around didn't *just* affect him. Sure, it was his baggage, but spending time with Faye meant making her carry it, too. He couldn't do that to anybody, especially her. He'd watched for a week as the story had grown and spread like wildfire, until people would whisper as he walked by, or stop talking abruptly when he entered a room. He wondered if Faye was receiving the same backlash, and guessed for her, it might have been worse. So, when he'd received the email from Bob asking him to volunteer at the town's Holiday Festival to man the Elementary School's annual donation table, he had no choice but to answer with a resounding *no*.

That had all been fine, until he'd received the second email from the Superintendent begging him to reconsider. He'd managed to politely decline that, too, but once he received an email from the Mayor of Pine Grove less asking him and more instructing him... well, he couldn't exactly turn her down, could he? Like it or not, it looked like Faye would be stuck with him.

Dylan climbed out of the driver's seat of his new pickup truck and circled around to the back, opening up the tailgate and sliding out cases of maple hardwood flooring he'd ordered from the local hardware store. The pickup truck wasn't *technically* new, but it was new to him. He'd seen the red Chevy parked on a front lawn with a For Sale sign propped up on the dashboard. Needing a vehicle capable of hauling, he'd knocked on the owner's door and offered him $800 cash on the spot. The truck wasn't his BMW Z4, but it was much more practical.

A twinge in his knee caused him to double over, and one of the cases fell to the ground. *Dammit*, he winced, hoping he hadn't just wrecked a couple hundred dollars' worth of flooring. He lowered himself to the pavement and massaged his knee, wondering when exactly the hell he'd gotten so *old*. What was next, he'd develop a hunchback?

A familiar baritone drew him back to reality.

"I would have thought retirement was fun, but you look like you've just got an ass-full of snow."

Dylan's head snapped up and he laughed, unable to contain the grin spreading across his face at the sight of his friend.

"Marcus!" He yelled, climbing to his feet and throwing one arm around the man's stocky, 5'11" frame before giving him a fist-bump. "What the heck are you doing here?"

"Can't a guy pop in on an old friend?" Marcus asked.

"Not in the middle of training season, he can't." Dylan said, the excitement in his voice morphing into concern, peppered with suspicion. "What are you doing here, Marcus? I'm happy to see you, don't get me wrong, but surely your coach didn't give you a pass during the most important few weeks of training."

Marcus hung his head, but the smirked remained. The knot forming in Dylan's gut intensified.

"Maybe my coach just has enough faith in my skills, he thought I could afford some time off," Marcus said, giving Dylan a playful punch in the shoulder. He wore a wide grin, but Dylan could see there was something else lurking behind his eyes.

"What's really going on, Marcus?"

Marcus raked a hand over his grown-out buzz cut, then shrugged his shoulders.

"I'm aging out," he said, a tinge of sadness darkening his usually affable demeanor. "My coach keeps telling me I'm good, that I've got plenty of time left, but I can already tell. The competition keeps getting younger, and judges have seen it all from me already. I think…" he paused, looking down at his snow boots. "I think I need to do something new. Something a little more permanent."

Dylan blinked at him, desperately trying to make sense of everything he'd just heard. He understood where Marcus was coming from. Once Dylan had hit 30, a majority of the publicity he received had revolved around his age compared to the rest of his competition. Even his career-ending injury, a product of icy weather conditions and too much bravado, had been attributed to his age at the time. But despite it all, he hadn't let the talk about his age bother him. It surprised him that Marcus would.

"I hear you, but are you sure you gave this enough thought?" Dylan asked. "I retired because I didn't have a choice. You've still got so many good runs left in you."

Marcus scoffed and rolled his eyes, and Dylan stiffened, narrowing his eyes at his friend. They'd had plenty of words over Dylan's decision to retire before Marcus had come around to the idea. With Dylan's injury, though, the choice had been a no-brainer. For Marcus, this was all just out of the blue. He was just looking out for his friend.

"You had a choice," Marcus said. "And you chose the future that ended the best for you and your family. I'm just trying to do the same thing."

Dylan didn't, *couldn't*, believe that the story ended there. However, he was excited to see him, and he wasn't interested in spending time arguing when they had so much catching up to do. He decided he would let it go for now, but he'd have to talk to Marcus about it again soon, before it was too late.

Marcus helped Dylan carry the bundles of hardwood flooring from the truck to the house, admiring the battered old Victorian and the recently renovated kitchen. A light snow had begun to fall, dusting the ground a soft, bright white. Neither one of them spoke, the weight of their earlier conversation hanging heavily in the air. Finally, once all of the bundles were placed in their respective rooms, Dylan led Marcus into the great room, a living area toward the front of the house with a large stone fireplace. Removing a few logs from a basket next to the fireplace, Dylan quickly got a fire started so that they could thaw out a little.

"So," Dylan said, rubbing his hands together in front of the flames. "When you say you want to do something more permanent... what did you have in mind?"

Marcus looked around at the room, at the primed walls and exposed subfloor, and shrugged his shoulders.

"Something like this, maybe."

Dylan looked around, his brows knitting together in confusion.

"You want to buy a house?"

"I want to do renovations," Marcus said. "I want to take something old, like this house, and make it new again. I'm thinking about starting my own business."

"Wow, Marcus, that's a great idea," Dylan said, surprised to hear that Marcus wanted to do anything besides tear up a half-pipe. "What brought that on?"

"I was trying to think of what I wanted to do when I finished competing. I realized that I wanted to create something I could pass down as a legacy one day. My future kids aren't going to care about medals and trophies. A business that they can be a part of, though? That's a real legacy."

Dylan was speechless in the face of his friend's plan. He himself hadn't put too much thought into what came next. He knew he needed to settle Ben in, and finish renovating the house. After that. . . well, he didn't really know. Every time he tried to think about what kind of career he wanted, he drew a blank. He'd defined himself in two ways: first, as a snowboarder. After Ben came along, he became a father, too. Outside of those two things, he didn't really know what- or *who-* he was.

"Sounds like a great plan," Dylan said. "Let me know if there's anything I can do to help."

"Well actually," Marcus said, his determined gaze turning sheepish. Dylan cocked a curious eyebrow. "I was hoping you might want to go into business with me."

Marcus' words were like a punch to the gut, knocking the wind out of him. A business? Dylan felt honored that Marcus wanted to be his business partner, and include him in the legacy he wanted to build. Dylan liked the work well enough, too. But starting a business from scratch? That would be a lot of time, and a lot of work, and Dylan's plan had been to settle down. It was a risk.

"I'll have to think about it," Dylan said, not meeting Marcus' eyes. "As much as I'd love to, I have a lot of work to do on this house, and I want to make sure Ben is settled and happy. But if you're still offering in the future, I'll definitely think about it."

"Calm down, man," Marcus said, laughing and shaking his head. "I'm not planning on drawing up letters of incorporation tomorrow. Take some time and think it over, and get back to me when you're ready."

Dylan nodded, the idea rooting itself deep in the back of his mind. He would love to start his own business. Now just wasn't the right time.

"Will do," he muttered.

"Alright," Marcus said. "Now..." he turned around and gestured to the bundle of flooring beside them. "Did you want help laying this? I've got the afternoon free."

Dylan clapped him on the shoulder. "It's good to see you, man."

The hauled a few of the cases up the driveway and around to the front door, catching each other up on their lives since they'd last seen each other. Marcus was in the middle of telling him about his time in Aspen when a sporty white Audi screeched to a stop in front of Dylan's house. The men stopped and watched as a stiletto-heeled, knee-high leather boot swung out of the car, a tall, platinum blond woman climbing out shortly after.

Dylan felt all the air leave his lungs, like he'd been sucker punched right to the gut. *It couldn't be.* No, this was definitely not happening.

The woman flashed them a bright white smile as she sauntered up the driveway toward them with a familiar precision. One foot in front of the other, hips swaying with an exaggeration meant for the likes of Paris Fashion Week. He blinked his eyes shut, sure that when he opened them again, she would be gone.

He was wrong.

"Courtney, what the hell are you doing here?"

Chapter Eleven

Dylan stared at his ex is utter disbelief, trying to make sense of how she was standing mere inches from him, and in Pine Grove of all places. Contempt for the woman in front of him, the mother of his child, roiled inside of him like an angry storm on an open sea. What did she think she was doing just showing up after *five years* without so much as a damn postcard? They'd lived in the same state for years, and she hadn't ever bothered to see her child, not once! Now she was just going to show up on his doorstep out of the blue, like she had any right at all to be there? No way, Dylan was not about to let her barge in on their life, not when Ben was so close to settling in and having a normal life. He ground his teeth together to keep all the hateful words he felt from spilling out of him.

"You could at least try to look excited to see me," she said, her tone cool and detached.

Marcus let out a low whistle. "I'll, uh, be inside if you need me," he said, grabbing the case of flooring that Dylan held and scrambling inside. Dylan couldn't blame him for wanting to get away from Courtney as fast as he possibly could. He knew the feeling.

"How's Pablo, or Paco, or whatever the hell his name is?" Dylan asked, earning him a dramatic eye roll and heavy sigh. Last he'd heard, Courtney was hitting it big in the modeling world and living with her Italian photographer-turned-boyfriend. He'd found that out from a tabloid article, though. Courtney hadn't spoken to him since he watched her pack up her things in the middle of the night five years ago, and leave him and their toddler behind.

"*Paolo* is fine, he's shooting a campaign for Calvin Klein this week so he's pretty busy," she said, clearly not realizing that Dylan's question had been rhetorical. He snorted a laugh, and Courtney narrowed her eyes. "Do you have something to say? Because if so, you should just say it."

"Oh, there isn't enough time in the world to say what's on my mind," he said, brushing past her and walking toward the house. He called over his shoulder, "You wanna talk, I'll give you the name of my lawyer."

The clicking of heels behind him told him he was being followed. He stopped on the porch, just in front of the door, and watched with amusement as Courtney navigated the rickety wooden steps in her stilettos.

"Look, Dylan I just want to talk like adults. I literally came all the way from San Diego, the least you could do is give me like, five minutes," Courtney whined, crossing her arms in front of her and pouting like a child throwing a tantrum. He honestly couldn't remember what he'd ever seen in her.

"Two and a half minutes."

"I'll take it," she said, her voice growing softer and her eyes dropping to the ground. "Look I've just. . . I've been thinking a lot about Ben lately, and how much I've missed. How much I haven't been there for him. . ."

Dylan was not about to feel sympathetic for her, no way. Leaving was her choice, and he'd begged her not to go.

"You haven't been there for him at all," Dylan sniped.

"And I want to change that," Courtney said. "I know I can't make up for lost time, but I can make a promise to be there for him, now and in the future."

"Did you rehearse that on the flight over here?"

Dylan turned away from her and began to open the door, but stopped when he felt a hand on his shoulder. He turned back around and saw tears in her eyes, and for a moment he felt a pang of sympathy for her.

"I'm just asking for a chance."

The sound of a car door slamming caused them both to turn and look down the driveway. Dylan's heart sank when he saw Iris letting Ben out of her car, and the confused look on Ben's face as they made their way toward him and Courtney. Dylan saw the glint of recognition pass over his son's face, the confusion that morphed into surprise, then again into guarded suspicion. It broke his heart.

"Benny!" Courtney exclaimed, bending down to be eye level with him as he walked up to her. Dylan watched as Ben's steps slowed, and he stopped a few feet from Courtney and her outstretched arms. Ben looked from Courtney, to Dylan, and then back to Courtney, as if he couldn't decide if the woman he sort of recognized could be trusted. "Benny it's me, it's mommy!" Courtney said, her voice desperate, as if she was trying to convince him. Ben looked back to Dylan once more, before darting around them both running into the house.

Courtney hesitated for a moment, still crouched down low, and wrapped her arms around herself. When she finally stood up and turned around, Dylan could see the devastation written all over her face. Despite his better judgment, he reached out a hand and squeezed her arm sympathetically.

"He'll come around," Dylan said. "It might just take some time."

Courtney swiped at her cheeks, and fixed Dylan with a pathetic, doe-eyed look that, five years ago, might have won him over.

"So you'll give me a chance?" she asked, punctuating the words with hiccups and sniffles.

"Courtney. . ."

"Look I don't want it to come to this, but I've been talking to a lawyer, and. . ."

"You've been talking with a lawyer?" Dylan asked, his blood running cold and his vision going blurry. He whirled on her, the sudden rage he felt taking over completely. "You haven't been in his life for five years, Courtney. You left, never contacted us again until right now, and you think you have the right to go to a lawyer because, what, you think Ben will make for a good Instagram picture? Christ, Courtney."

"No, it's not like that, I just..."

"You just what? Thought you couldn't come talk to me without getting a lawyer involved? Thought the fact that you've been gone for the last five years might make me skeptical of you wanting to be back in Ben's life? Well, maybe you're right."

He flung open the front door and started inside, blinking away the anger that had bubbled up inside of him like a volcano ready to erupt.

"I will do it," she called after him. "I don't want to, but if it's the only way I can see my son again, Dylan, I'll do it."

He felt cornered, trapped. Like any control he had over his life had just been ripped away. What other choice did he have, other than to give in to what she wanted?

He looked back at her, hoping the contempt in his eyes mirrored the contempt he felt for her in that moment.

"Fine," Dylan said, biting back the bile that burned in his throat. "There's no need for lawyers. Just give me a few days, and let me talk to Ben. He's probably very confused, and today's not a great day for this anyway. I have to install the new flooring in the house, and Marcus is able to help this afternoon."

"Okay," she murmured, nodding her head so quickly, it made Dylan dizzy. "Maybe we can get lunch or something together."

"Fine. I'll call you."

"Alright."

Seemingly appeased for the moment, she made her way quickly back to her car, and gave Dylan one last glance before climbing in and driving off.

When he could no longer see her car, he raised his fist and slammed it into the porch railing, knocking loose one of the spindles.

"Shit," he thought, running a hand through his hair. So much for starting over in Pine Grove. His past was just determined to follow him wherever he went.

Marcus bounded out the front door and immediately eyed the broken piece of porch railing.

"What can I do?" Marcus asked, and Dylan just sighed. That was Marcus, always wanting to lend a hand. He thought for a moment, pacing on the porch, the anger and anxiety coursing through him making it difficult to stand still.

"Can you watch Ben for a little bit?"

"Yeah, of course," Marcus said. "Whatever you need."

"Thank you. I'll only be an hour or so."

Dylan bounded down the driveway to his truck, his mind racing. As he climbed into the cab, he didn't know if what he was about to do was smart, or stupid, or just plain insane. He didn't care. There was only one place he could think of going where he would be able to clear his head, one person he could talk to who might give him the honesty he desperately needed right now.

He started the engine, peeled out of the driveway, and headed straight for Faye's house.

PERHAPS THE ONLY THING Faye had inherited from her mother was the compulsion to clean when she was stressed. Bob had let her know that Dylan would be helping out at the Festival after all, and she hadn't been able to stop moving since. So far, she had completely scrubbed her kitchen from top to bottom, rearranged her closet by color and season, and bleached every surface in her bathroom. She was shoveling out her driveway from the prior nights blanket of fresh snow when a red pick-up truck stopped in front of her house.

Her knees nearly buckled when Dylan climbed out of the driver's side and started up the driveway toward her. What on earth was he doing here?

He probably wanted to set her straight about the Festival table, and make sure she knew that it didn't mean anything. Her stomach twisted into a knot. Was he going to want to talk about the article, too? Make sure she knew that he absolutely did *not* think of her in that way? She sucked in a deep breath, leaning her shovel against the garage, and putting on her best poker face as he approached.

"Hi, Faye."

"Hello," she said, doing the best she could to keep her tone cool and even. Her eyes raked over his face, and she realized that he looked... upset. Worried, even.

He kept his eyes fixed on the ground, grinding a toe into the hard packed snow still covering a large part of her driveway, refusing to meet her gaze. This was way worse than she thought.

"Look, if you're here about the article, or the festival, let me just save you the trouble," she said, wringing her hands on front of her. She'd clearly gotten his attention, because his head snapped up and he looked right at her. Her breath hitched when their eyes met, and she almost forgot what she was about to say.

"What do you mean?" He asked, and she noticed her hands were shaking.

Focus. "I know it doesn't mean anything, and that it's all just gossip. I know the Festival will be good publicity. You don't have to worry about me wanting anything from you, other than a few hours of your time working the donation table."

The concern on his face twisted into confusion, and Faye could feel her face getting hot, even in the icy winter cold.

"I'm not sure I understand what you're talking about."

"That's why you're here, isn't it? To make sure I don't get the wrong idea?"

"The wrong idea about what?" he asked.

Was she really going to have to spell it out for him? "The article about us being. . ." She hesitated, struggling to say it out loud. "Together."

He shook his head, laughing in a way that unnerved her. Something was clearly wrong.

"That's actually not why I'm here," he said. "I need some advice, from someone I can trust. Courtney - Ben's mother - she showed up at the house today," Dylan said.

Faye felt all manner of speech leave her brain. If she'd felt like an idiot before...

"Oh," was the only thing her brain could manage. They stared at each other for moment, a heavy and uncomfortable silence hanging between them. Finally, she asked, "Do you want to come inside for a minute?"

He nodded and followed her into the house, both of them stopping in the foyer to kick off their boots and remove their coats.

"Would you like some tea, or coffee or anything?" she asked, padding through the living room and into the kitchen. Dylan followed.

"Sure, whatever you're having," he said.

Faye grabbed the kettle off the stove and filled it with water, then put it back on the burner to heat up. As she pulled two mugs down from a cabinet and dropped a tea bag in each, she glanced over at Dylan, who was leaning against her kitchen table, arms crossed over his chest, watching her.

"So I take it you weren't expecting your ex to stop by?" Faye asked, eying him curiously.

"I haven't seen or heard from her in five years, and suddenly she just. . . shows up out of nowhere," he said.

"How did Ben take that?" she asked. She couldn't imagine it had gone well. She figured as young as Ben had been when his mother had left, he'd probably barely recognized her. Dylan's mouth flattened into a tight line.

"Not good," he said. "He was pretty confused."

"What did she want?"

"She wants to be a part of Ben's life," he said, his face darkening. "And she came prepared with lawyers."

"Lawyers? Without even talking to you first?"

He looked up at her, and Faye could see the pain in his eyes. She couldn't imagine how he must feel, wondering if he was going to lose his son to a woman who had abandoned them both so long ago. She wondered what had suddenly made Ben's mother have a change of heart, and for Ben's sake, she hoped it was genuine. She couldn't stand to think of what it would do to him if Courtney abandoned him a second time.

"She didn't think I would be receptive to it," he spat, his tone venomous. Snickering, he added, "She was right."

The kettle began to whistle, and Faye poured the hot water into the mugs. She dropped a teaspoon of sugar into each and gently stirred.

"And you want to know what you should do next?" she asked.

He nodded solemnly, his mouth a tight line. "I'm so worried she'll try to take him from me," he said, the words barely above a whisper. Faye's heart broke.

"My honest opinion," she started, Dylan looking at her intently, "is that there isn't a lot you can do right now. She's his mother, and as selfish or irresponsible as she might be, she has a right to see him and be in his life." She could sense Dylan becoming agitated at her honesty, so she added, "but I also don't think you should worry. You're an excellent father, and you've done everything you can to make sure Ben has a safe, happy, and healthy life. No sane judge would ever take him away from you. She can make whatever threats she wants, but at the end of the day. . . She might be his biological mother, but you're his parent. Nothing can change that."

He smiled, his eyes glassy. "Thank you."

Faye walked one of the mugs over to Dylan and he wrapped his hand around it, his fingers brushing against her hand and sending a bolt of electricity through her. She lifted her eyes to his, taking an unsteady breath as he circled his thumb over hers. The rough calluses on his skin sent shivers up and down her spine, and as he held her gaze, she wondered if it was possible she was imagining the sparks between them in that moment. She'd spent the last few days chastising herself for foolishly thinking there was something between them, for being so disappointed that he'd canceled their weekly meetings, and now...

"Well," she said, her throat suddenly dry and her voice husky. "If there's anything I can do to help, let me know."

He didn't say anything, he only took the mug and set it on the table behind him, never taking his eyes off of hers. In one swift movement he closed the gap between them, sealing his lips on hers in a frenzy of heat and need that stole the air right out of her lungs. Her surprise evaporated as one of his hands found her waist and pulled her in closer, the other tangling itself in her hair, and she gave in to the kiss completely. She wrapped her arms around his neck, letting herself get lost in the feeling of his body so close to hers. She kissed him back, terrified that it might end just as suddenly as it had begun, and she didn't want it to end, not now, not ever. Without ever taking his lips from hers, Dylan steered her a few steps backward until they reached the kitchen counter. With hardly any effort at all, he lifted her up and she gasped as her feet left the floor, her backside finding the countertop. She pulled him in closer, her hands raking through his hair as she wrapped her legs around him and prayed that this moment, this perfect moment she'd felt like she'd waited her entire life for, would never end.

When he finally removed his lips from hers, she wanted to protest. She wanted to grab a fistful of his shirt and pull him back to her, but she didn't. Instead, she waited as he rested his forehead against hers, his breathing heavy and erratic. She inhaled the musky, woodsy scent of his cologne, and fought the urge to throw herself at him again. She felt his hand brush her chin, and he lifted it up until she was looking right in his eyes.

"Faye," he breathed, stroking her hair, and her cheek. Suddenly, he pulled back and raked a hand through his hair, leaving her sitting on the counter. "I'm so sorry," he said. "I don't know what came over me, I. . ."

"Don't be sorry," Faye interrupted. "I wanted it, too."

He smiled, and she laughed nervously as they let what had just happened settle between them.

"I should, uh, probably get back to Ben," Dylan said. "Marcus is watching him right now, and we've got some flooring to lay."

"Sure," Faye said, carefully sliding off the countertop and walking him toward the door. He put on his coat and his boots, and turned to face her, taking a few steps closer until he was just a few inches from her. He winked, and then bent down and gently brushed his lips against hers again.

"Thank you," he murmured.

"For what?"

He gave her a Cheshire cat smile. "For being you."

He slipped out the front door, and Faye watched him leave from the window. Once his truck disappeared around the corner, she let out a long exhale. Two things were now overwhelmingly apparent: First, she wasn't crazy. Second. . . She definitely, absolutely, undoubtedly was in a whole mess of trouble.

Chapter Twelve

"And then, after Venice, we went and saw the Leaning Tower of... Dylan? Are you listening?"

Courtney snapped her finger in front of Dylan's face, drawing him out of his daydream. She and Ben were staring at him, and he tried to recall what Courtney had been talking about. *Something about gondolas, maybe? Venice?* That's right, her trip to Italy with Pablo, or Paolo, or whatever his name was. They were having a light lunch together at Chloe's Coffeehouse, and Courtney had been spending the whole time trying to impress Ben with stories of her world travels. If she was trying to impress Dylan, too, he wouldn't know it. He was distracted, his mind far away in Faye's kitchen, replaying the previous evening. He had barely slept a wink, spending the night tossing and turning as visions of Faye with her hands in his hair danced in his head. It had taken every ounce of willpower he had to pull himself away from her. It would take a lot more than that to keep him away from her. He'd opened a *massive* Pandora's box when he'd decided to kiss Faye Parker.

"Yes, sorry," he grunted, redirecting his attention to Courtney and her lavish stories. He caught Chloe eying him from behind the counter, her scowl suggesting she wasn't a fan of he and Ben's new companion, and he wondered what, if anything Faye had told her. Did she know? Did she approve? Wait, why did he care if Chloe approved? *She's Faye's best friend*, he told himself. *Her approval is everything.*

He listened to Courtney drone on and on about all the exotic places her boyfriend had taken her over the past year, frowning at how enthralled with her stories their son looked. Ben was on the edge of his seat, swinging his legs back and forth, his eyes wide and fixed directly on his mother. He supposed it was good that Ben was no longer afraid of his mother, but he hated that they might be setting Ben up for disappointment.

The door to the cafe swung open, the bell above the door jingling, and Dylan's pulse quickened. Faye walked through the door brushing snow off of her jacket, her hair a wild mass of curls underneath a red beanie. She stopped dead in her tracks when she saw him, her face blushing the color of her hat, and gave him a small wave. He smiled and waved back, the memory of his hands on her hips, her back, in her hair, replaying in his mind for the millionth time.

Courtney snapped her fingers at him again.

"Can you stop doing that?" he snapped, taking her by surprise. She leaned back in her chair and folded her arms across her chest. He watched her look toward the door, her eyes following Faye over to the counter, where she was greeting Chloe.

"Oh, I get it now," Courtney said wryly, narrowing her eyes at Dylan. "I guess the tabloids weren't kidding."

"Leave it alone," he growled. "It's none of your business."

"Does it involve Ben? Because if so, then it *is* my business."

He rolled his eyes and shook his head, unable to contain the laughter that bubbled out of him.

"Well then that makes Paolo my business," Dylan countered.

"Excuse me, but my relationship with Paolo is - "

"No," Dylan spat. "Parenting is a two-way street, Courtney. No double standards."

She looked away from him, her arms still crossed, and her lips pursed. The three of them sat in silence until Faye strolled over, a large coffee in one hand and her hat in another. Her eyes never strayed from Dylan.

"Hi," she said, a small smirk tugging at the corner of her lips. What Dylan wouldn't do to brush his finger across them.

"Miss Parker!" Ben said, jumping up from his chair and throwing his arms around her legs. Dylan watched while Courtney's face grew more and more grim the more she saw Faye interacting with their son.

Ben turned to Courtney proudly. "This is my teacher," he announced.

"Yes, I've heard all about your new teacher," Courtney sneered, and Dylan had to fight the urge to whisk Faye out of the cafe and back to the safety of her house. *Where they could be alone*, his brain reminded him. He pushed the thoughts away, knowing he wouldn't be able to concentrate if he let them continue.

"Faye, this is Courtney, Ben's mother," he said, watching as the two women stared each other down. As expected, Faye was the first to extend the olive branch, and her hand.

"It's nice to meet you," she said, but Courtney didn't shake her hand. Faye awkwardly pulled it back, and Dylan glared at his ex, who was doing her best to appear indifferent. Faye continued to try and make peace. "How long are you in town?" she asked.

"As long as I have to be," Courtney replied curtly, staring daggers at Dylan. He shot them right back at her.

"Well I hope you'll get the stay for the Holiday Festival," Faye said. "It's the biggest Festival of the year, and it's a really fun time."

Courtney turned her venomous glare up to Faye. "Small towns are so... *Interesting*," she said, clearly meaning as an insult. She looked back at Dylan. "Will you and Ben be attending this *Festival*?"

"Well actually," Dylan started, worried that he was about to open a can of worms that might never be closed again. "I'm going to be volunteering at the Festival."

"Oh, is that so?" Courtney asked. He nodded.

"With Faye," he added, hoping it was as much of a jab as he intended it to be. He watched Courtney's face go blank, her lips pursing.

"And who will be watching Ben while you're," she flicked her eyes from Dylan, to Faye, and then back to Dylan, "*volunteering.*"

"His babysitter agreed to watch him at the festival for a few hours," Dylan spat. "He'll be fine."

Courtney's face softened, and she turned to Ben, mussing his curly hair.

"Would you like to hang out at the festival with mommy, sweetie?" she asked him. Dylan's stomach twisted into a knot as he watched Ben's eyes light up.

"Sure!" Ben squealed, and Courtney turned a victorious smirk on Dylan.

"Then it's settled," she said. "I'll take care of our son, while you're off doing. . ." She looked at Faye. "Whatever it is you need to do."

Faye's face was a bright scarlet, and Dylan felt like the biggest jackass in the world. He felt the urge to jump up and defend her, to tell Courtney to go pound sand, but he was terrified that he might make things between them worse. If he wasn't careful, he might make Courtney get some lawyer involved who will try to take his son away. Faye cleared her throat, punctuating the awkward silence that had settled over the table.

"Well, I have to get going. It was nice to meet you, Courtney," she said, abruptly turning to leave. Dylan shot Courtney a pointed look, before jumping up and following Faye out of the cafe.

"Faye!" he called after her, jogging to catch up to her. She stopped and turned around, her face still tinged pink with embarrassment. He hung his head.

"I'm so sorry," he said. "She's a witch. I should have told her to go to Hell."

"No," Faye insisted. "I understand. You don't want to rock the boat."

He nodded, grateful that she could be so understanding after Courtney had been such a troll to her. He closed the few inches between them, lifted his hand to her cheek, and rubbed his thumb over the warm, pink skin, slowly drawing a line down her cheek and under her chin. His breath hitched in his throat as her eyes fluttered closed, and he tilted her head up toward him, gently placing his lips on hers. She sighed into him, and before he could lose himself in her again, he pulled back.

He couldn't explain the need to be near her, to reach out and touch her. He only knew that the closer he got to her, the closer he wanted to be. The last week, they'd spent whatever free time they could find together, and somehow it never felt like enough. Just as suddenly as it had started, he found himself unable to get Faye off his mind. And he didn't want to.

"I'll see you at the festival," he said, and she smiled. The Holiday festival wasn't for another few days, and he hoped he could make it until then. He had renovations to finish, and she had school and homework to grade before Christmas... Maybe he would find some time to sneak away and see her before then.

"See you then," she said, squeezing his hand before disappearing down the street. He turned to go back into the cafe, and nearly ran into Chloe, who was standing by the door with her hands on her hips, a disapproving look on her face. He stuffed his hands into his pockets.

"I'm guessing she's, uh, mentioned..."

"If you hurt her," Chloe said, narrowing her eyes, "I will hurt you. Do I make myself clear?"

He swallowed hard. "Crystal."

"Good," she said. "Now get back inside and get that debutante out of my cafe. She's driving away all my customers."

Chloe turned on her heel and huffed back into the cafe. Dylan followed her, and was immediately met with Courtney's unmistakable stink eye. She stood up abruptly and gathered her things.

"Can we go now?" she asked. "I have an appointment to go get my nails done across the street and I need to make sure they actually know what a powder dip is."

Dylan rolled his eyes, he and Ben following Courtney out of the cafe. He gave Chloe a week smile as they left, which she didn't return, and he thought if he could get through this, he could probably get through anything.

Chapter Thirteen

Faye arrived early on the Saturday of the festival to set up the table with the other vendors. Main Street in town along the lake had been closed down, and almost every business in town had their own table or booth set up. She was next to Brigsby's Books' booth this year, where Melvin Brigsby would be hosting regularly scheduled children's story times throughout the day. He'd shown his selections - a Dr. Seuss book, one by Eric Carle, and a popular story by Crockett Johnson, *Harold and the Purple Crayon*. Melvin told Faye he'd make sure after every story time to mention her donation table to any parents around, and she had a feeling it would work out perfectly. The Elementary School's donation table was simple - just one long table, with bins underneath labeled for every type of school supply they usually received donations for. Faye also like to hand out fliers citing previous years' donations, and information about other local schools they were able to help out. Now in its fourth year, they didn't have to do much advertising to make the supply drive a success. This year, however, the table would be manned by none other than Pine Grove's own Olympic snowboarder, and Faye had a feeling they were going to have their best year yet.

A few minutes before Mayor Albright was scheduled to say a few words and officially declare this year's Holiday Festival to begin, Principal Griffin ambled over to the table, a look of panic on his face. As he approached the table, adjusting the thick scarf around his next and the blue beanie covering his balding head, he looked all around, then back at Faye.

"Where's Dylan?" he asked. "Shouldn't he be here by now?"

Faye laughed. "I'm sure he'll be here soon; the festival hasn't even started yet. Don't worry."

As if on cue, she spotted Dylan making his way toward them, Ben and Courtney in tow. Bob let out a whimper at the sight of the tall, lithe model wearing her signature scowl.

"Is she going to be at the table, too? Because I think that might hinder our cause more than help it," he said.

Faye shook her head. "She wouldn't be caught dead," she assured him. "She's going to watch Ben while Dylan helps out."

"Oh, good," he sighed, plastering on a big smile as the three of them stopped in front of the table.

Courtney looked around at the table, her face scrunching like she'd smelled something foul.

"You expect to get people's donations with a table like this?" Courtney asked. "Where are the streamers and balloons? The little 'Thank You' gifts? The little placards you can write your name on when you give?"

Dylan snickered. "Relax, it's a school supply drive, not the Met Gala."

She huffed and turned up her nose, surveying the other nearby booths with similar disdain. Bob clapped his hands together.

"Well, now that the dream team is here," he said, giving them both a conspiratorial wink, "let's bring home the gold on this year's donations!"

Faye rolled her eyes, but Dylan gave Bob a high-five.

"I left my classroom unlocked, so we'll just bring the donations in once the festival is over," she told him. Bob gave them both a thumbs up, then left to check out the other booths and tables. Ben pulled on the sleeve of Courtney's black suede parka, pointing down the road toward a local popcorn stand.

"Mommy, can we get kettle corn?" he asked.

"Sure, darling!" she cooed, bending over to ruffle Ben's hair. She straightened and turned to Dylan and Faye. "We're going to walk around for a while," she announced. "Hopefully, I'll find something to eat other than carnival food."

Dylan gave Ben a kiss on the forehead before they ambled off, and Faye let a little snort of laughter escape her when Courtney was out of earshot.

"She's a little out of her element," Faye said.

"You think?" Dylan replied sarcastically. He wrapped her up in his arms and planted a long, hot kiss on her mouth.

When he finally released her, she found herself gasping for air. "What was that for?" she asked, unable to control the smile that had spread from ear to ear.

"Just missed you, is all," he said, and she knew the feeling. The last few days had been incredibly busy, and she hadn't had much time to accomplish anything besides work and grading report cards, much less to sneak away to see Dylan. They'd seen each other in passing, but never for longer than a few minutes, and *never* alone.

Melvin Brigsby cleared his throat at the table next door. "You lovebirds behave now, ya hear?" he chuckled.

"Yes, sir," Dylan promised, and Faye beamed. The watched as Mayor Albright approached the stage in the middle of the street, where later local bands would play music and carolers would sing Christmas carols. The town gathered around as she said a few words about the town, and the spirit of Christmas, and then formally declared the festival as begun. A cheer rippled through the crowd, and everyone dispersed to enjoy the festival's many activities and booths.

Two hours later, Faye could not believe her eyes. Most of the donation bins were filled, and the festival still had several hours left before it ended around sunset. They'd had a constant line of people with bags of donated school supplies, all of whom were stopping to talk with Dylan. A few even asked for autographs or selfies, which he happily obliged, and Faye's heart was filled with gratitude. She began to tally up the numbers of supplies in each bin, counting the individual notebooks, packs of pencils, and boxes of crayons until she realized something incredible. *They'd already blown past last year's numbers.* Two hours in, and they'd already blown last year's numbers out of the water. She could hardly believe her eyes.

She showed Dylan, and they high-fived, except he didn't let go of her hand. He gave it a little squeeze, and she delighted in the rush of warmth she felt spread from her hand all the way down to her toes.

A few minutes later, man with a camera approached the table, and Faye felt her stomach knot into a ball. Another tabloid magazine? She could feel her palms getting clammy, and saw the concern that crossed Dylan's face.

"Excuse me," the photographer said. "I'm with the Syracuse Times, and we'd like to do a feature on your donation table. Can I get a quick photo?"

Relief washed over her, and she looked at Dylan and shrugged.

"Sure." The two of them posed together with the donation boxes while the photographer snapped a few pictures, then thanked them and handed Faye a business card.

"An editor will be reaching out, but would you mind sending an email to this address with where further donations can be sent?" he asked. "We want to publicize in the paper, so that anyone who reads the Syracuse Times will be able to submit a donation if they want."

Faye's jaw hit the floor. "Yes, of course!" she said. "Thank you!"

The photographer moved on, but Faye still couldn't believe it. If they continued to get donations even after the festival, they could supply an entire other school district! So many kids would no longer have to worry about whether or not they could get new pencils or notebooks, or worry about using up their erasers. Her eyes filled with tears, and she turned to Dylan.

"Thank you," she said. "I'm not sure this would have happened without you being involved."

Dylan didn't say anything, but just leaned in and kissed her on the forehead. He cleared his throat when he saw Ben approaching with Courtney, who looked even more miserable than normal.

"I'm *exhausted*," she said, sighing dramatically and taking a seat behind the donation table. "I simply cannot walk around anymore."

"Did you want to go back to the house?" Dylan offered, pulling out the keys to his truck. "I'm sure Faye could give us a ride home once the festival is over, if you'd like."

Courtney gagged. "You expect me to drive that rickety old truck? I don't think so. No, why don't the two of you take a quick break? Benny and I will watch the donation table, and you guys can go enjoy the festival."

Faye nearly choked, she was so surprised by the offer. She could tell Dylan was just as surprised as she was.

"Seriously?" he asked, and Courtney shrugged.

"Sure, why not. You guys look like you could use a break, and anyway, how hard can it be? You just put the stuff in the boxes."

Faye looked pleadingly at Dylan. She *could* use a break, and she wouldn't mind getting to spend a few minutes alone with him enjoying the festival. He seemed to read her mind.

"Okay, if you're sure," he said. "Thank you. We'll just go grab something to eat, we won't be long."

"Good luck," Courtney glowered, "unless you actually *like* corn dogs and cheese fries."

They set off down the road to check out the Festival activities, her hand in his, their fingers interlocked. She liked the way it felt, his hand, warm and slightly rough, engulfing hers. She paid no attention to the looks they got from people they walked past, and instead just focused on enjoying the time they had together. It had been a long, long time since she'd done anything but man the donation table at the Festival, and it was nice to be on the other side for once.

They decided to stop at Chloe's booth first, where she was selling coffee and hot chocolate to go. As they got closer, Faye noticed that Chloe was *not* running the booth by herself. Right next to her, taking orders and handing out drinks while Chloe prepped them and replenished the coffee, was David. Faye leaned into Dylan and quickly explained the fact that Chloe was practically in love with David before they got close enough to hear.

"Two hot chocolates, please," Dylan ordered. David took their payment and, after squinting at Dylan, appeared to recognize him.

"Hey! You're the guy!" he said, tapping Chloe on the shoulder. She turned and scowled at David, then at Dylan, and then grinned when she saw Faye.

"I heard your donations are already crushing last year's numbers," she said, coming around from behind the booth and wrapping her friend in a hug. "I am *so* proud of you."

"Thanks," Faye said, still unable to believe how successful they had been already. "It's pretty surreal, but I think we owe a lot of it to Dylan."

Dylan shook his head, but Chloe gave him a playful punch on the arm. "Nice work, Dylan. Thanks for making my best friend's cause a success." With a wink, she added, "Brownie points."

The took their hot chocolates and continued strolling, grabbing cinnamon sugar pretzels at one of the food trucks and perusing the Festival activities. They ran into Iris and Marcus Washington going head to head at the Ring Toss, and they stopped to watch as Iris scored the last ring, and beat her older brother.

"Yes!" she yelled, pumping her fist in the air, and then punching her brother in the arm. "You may be the athletic one, but I'm the family carnival games champion."

"Don't let it get to your head," Marcus teased, when he spotted Faye and Dylan watching. Faye had known the Washington's her whole life, and had gone to school with Marcus. She'd known he'd left town shortly after high school to pursue professional snowboarding, but as far as she knew, he hadn't quite hit it big yet. She'd heard he was in town to visit his sister, but hadn't put the pieces together that he and Dylan knew each other until he'd told her. She supposed it was inevitable they would cross paths during competition season, and Dylan had mentioned to her that they were close friends.

"Well, what do we have here?" Marcus asked, winking at Dylan and giving Faye a quick hug.

"Watch it," Dylan said, laughing and fist-bumping his friend.

"Faye, nice to see you," Marcus said.

"You too," she replied.

They chatted while Iris picked out her prize for winning the Ring Toss, and she joined the conversation with a large pink bear wearing a silver bow-tie.

"Dylan, how's Ben?" she asked. "I'm always free if the two of you are looking for a date night!"

Faye smiled, and Dylan laughed. "I might just take you up on that," he said.

They talked for a little while longer, Dylan filling Marcus in on the Courtney drama since they'd last spoken. After a few minutes, Iris turned to Marcus and put a hand on her hip.

"Bro, I'm starving," she said. "Can we please go get something to eat?"

"*Fine*, anything for my baby sister," Marcus said, shrugging and rolling his eyes. They said their goodbyes, and Dylan and Faye made their way toward the lake, walking along the water's edge before settling down on a bench where they could people watch and soak in the view. They finished their pretzels and drank their hot chocolate in silence, enjoying the view of the serene, ice-covered lake amid the boisterous atmosphere of the festival. Faye curled her knees up to her chest and rested her head on Dylan's shoulder, drinking in the absolute perfection of the moment. He put his arm around her and pulled her close, and she swore she might start purring, she was so comfortable and happy.

"So, I was thinking," Dylan whispered, his lips just above her ear. She shivered as his breath tickled her ear and neck, and squirmed closer to him. "What are you doing for Christmas this year?"

Faye sat up and looked at him. "Nothing in particular," she said. With her parents on their cruise, she didn't actually have any plans for Christmas Day. "Why?"

"Well," he said, turning to face her. He looked sheepish and nervous, but still so incredibly handsome. "I was hoping you would spend Christmas with Ben and I, if you aren't already busy."

She threw her arms around him and buried her face in his neck, hoping he wouldn't see the tears that were welling up in her eyes. She'd been so disappointed to spend Christmas alone, without her family, but now. . . Now, she had Dylan and Ben to spend Christmas with. To open presents with Christmas morning, and watch Christmas movies with all day. To eat Christmas cookies they'd baked and drink peppermint hot chocolate with. To start new traditions with. There was nothing she could think of that she wanted to do more.

"I would love that," she replied.

The sat there holding each other for a little while longer, until the setting sun in the distance told them they'd been gone for much longer than an hour.

"We should get back," Dylan said, rousing Faye off of the bench but pulling her in toward him. "I'm sure Courtney is going crazy by now."

They walked back to the donation table, hand in hand again, Faye basking in the glow of the perfect day the Festival had turned out to be. They slowed, however, as they got closer and saw a frantic Courtney, circling the nearby tables and booths, a look of pure panic on her face. Faye's pulse quickened as she scanned the area for Ben. She didn't see him. She felt Dylan's grip tighten, then let go of her hand completely as she strode quickly over to Courtney, who was talking to Melvin Brigsby and gesturing wildly.

"Courtney!" Dylan called as they got back to the table. She didn't react, instead still talking to Melvin as Faye and Dylan stopped just behind her. "Courtney what's going on?" he asked again. He got her attention this time, and she turned around. Her face, earlier perfectly painted with a full face of makeup, was now smeared and streaked with black mascara.

Was she crying? Faye's blood turned to ice. What on earth was going on?

Courtney mumbled something unintelligible between the sobs, and sniffles, and hiccups that just kept coming and coming like waves on the ocean, calm for a moment, then all at once. She buried her face in her hands, and Faye watched as Dylan went to her, putting his arm around her as he tried to calm her down. Faye looked around again, scanning the park, the booths, and the street for Ben, but still not seeing him. She turned back to Courtney and, as calmly as she could, asked her the question she feared was the cause of Courtney's panic.

"Courtney, where is Ben?"

Dylan's head snapped up, and he immediately took a survey of the surrounding area. When he didn't see Ben, his face went white as a sheet. He turned to Courtney, grabbed her by the shoulders, and gently shook her.

"Where is Ben, Courtney? What happened? What's going on?"

Courtney continued to sob, burying her head in her hands at the mention of Ben's name. While Dylan kept trying to get information out of her, Faye ran over to Melvin's booth to see what he might know.

"Did she say anything to you?" Faye asked Melvin, who looked at her gravely. "Did she say anything about Ben?"

Melvin shook his head. "Only that she couldn't find him," he said, confirming Faye's fear. Melvin looked around, then leaned in a little closer to her. "Between you and me, she wasn't really paying him much mind after you two left. She took a phone call, and it seemed to be pretty important."

Faye looked over at Dylan and Courtney, who was still sobbing uncontrollably, then back at Melvin. "Thanks, Mr. Brigsby," she said. She walked back over to Dylan, and pulled him aside.

"Melvin said Courtney was looking for Ben when we walked over," she told him. "Dylan, if Courtney isn't sure where he could be, I think we need to get the authorities involved."

Dylan's face was a pallid, gray color, as if he was going to get sick. He wouldn't look her in the eye. Instead, he whirled back around on his ex.

"Courtney, please tell us what's going on. Where is Ben? We can't help if you don't tell us what's happening."

Courtney turned her tearful eyes up toward Dylan and Faye, and sniffled. .

"Ben is gone," she sobbed. "He's gone, and I can't find him."

Chapter Fourteen

Dylan couldn't think. He couldn't move. He couldn't *breathe*. Ben was gone, missing, and he didn't even know where to start.

Guilt tore through him. Ben had walked off, disappeared, and where had Dylan been? Enjoying the festival with Faye, not thinking about anything or anyone but Faye. Not the paparazzi, not Courtney. Not Ben. How had he forgotten about his son? Why hadn't he been concerned with what his son was doing? Why had he just trusted Courtney to look out for him?

Courtney. He raked a hand through his hair, the anguish in his chest threatening to squeeze the life out of him. He should have known better than to trust the woman who'd abandoned them to watch over his son. Leaving her had been a stupid, stupid call.

"I'm gonna go find the Sheriff, see if he can lend a hand," Faye squeaked. She ran off, and Dylan turned to confront Courtney, who was now sitting on a chair, hugging her knees against her.

"What were you doing that you couldn't keep an eye on our son?" he growled. Courtney looked up at him with tearful eyes, and shook her head.

"I don't know, he was just there, and then... He wasn't."

She dropped her head into her hands, and Dylan couldn't control himself. He slammed his fist down on the table beside her, causing her to jump in her chair, and then start sobbing against.

"What were you doing that was so much more important than our son?" he bellowed, his heart racing and his vision blurring. Courtney rubber her eyes, but wouldn't look at him.

"I got a phone call," she whispered. "I took it, I was only not paying attention for like a few minutes, but when I hung up he was gone."

Dylan exhaled sharply. *How could she?* What could have possibly been so important that it had taken her attention away from Ben? *Hypocrite*, he chided himself, *just like you were too busy paying attention to Faye to worry about your son.*

"What was the call about?" he asked, knowing it wouldn't make a difference who she was talking to, or why. But still, he needed to know. He needed to know if his suspicion was right.

"What does that matter?" she asked.

"Just tell me who you were talking to."

Courtney took a deep breath, and still not meeting his gaze, whispered, "My manager."

Figures. Courtney had put work before her son, again.

"How long was the call?" he asked.

"What does that have to do - "

"How long were you not paying attention to our son?" The rational part of his brain knew that she hadn't done this on purpose. But the other part of his brain? The emotional, animal part that was consumed with fear and rage over not knowing where Ben was - that part blamed her.

"Maybe half an hour," she muttered.

"Half an hour? What the hell were you talking about for half a God damn hour, Courtney?"

"A gig."

Before he had the chance to lay into her over it, Faye walked back over to them, Sheriff O'Neil in tow. She gave him a small, sympathetic smile, and he closed his eyes, wanting to tell her he appreciated her being there for him, but just not being able to find the energy or the words. He needed to focus all of his energy on finding Ben. *That* had to be his priority right now.

"Are you the parents?" Sheriff O'Neil asked, addressing Dylan and Courtney. They both nodded, and the Sheriff pulled out a notepad and pen from his pocket. "Alright, well the best thing we can do in this situation is remain calm. I'm going to ask you both some questions, get a description out to law enforcement of your boy, and then we'll get as many officers out into the town as it takes find him. Sound like a plan to you?"

Courtney hiccupped, and they both nodded again. They described Ben to the Sheriff, his height, his hair, and eye color, what he was wearing. He asked them what nicknames he responded to, if he had any close friends, and whether it was possible he might be with one of them. The whole time, Dylan couldn't get past the fact that he felt like he was watching everything unfold from outside his body. He was numb as he described Dylan's shoes in great detail, in case his clothes were somehow covered or changed, and whether or not he had any birthmarks. It felt like a nightmare, the sort of thing you see happen all the time on TV, but never expect to happen to you.

"About how long has it been since you realized he was missing?" the Sheriff asked. Everyone turned to look at Courtney.

"About forty-five minutes, I guess," she sniffled. The sheriff scribbled in his notepad, then sighed heavily.

"Now, don't take this the wrong way," he said, his eyes flicking between Courtney and Dylan, "but is there anything going on that would cause him to run away? We don't want to rule anything out, but it's not uncommon for a kid to get upset and think that running away will teach their parents a lesson."

"No way," Dylan said, shaking his head. Ben would not just run away and scare his parents half to death. He was a good kid, with a good head on his shoulders. He looked at Courtney for support, but the guilt on her face told a different story.

"Well. . ." She murmured, getting the Sheriff's attention. "When I was on the phone, he overheard me talking. He got a little upset."

Dylan rounded on her. "Why would he get upset?" he asked.

"Because of the gig my manager called me about," she Courtney started. "It's in London, and they want me to fly out tomorrow night.

Ben asked me. . ." She stifled a sob, "he asked me if I was going to leave again."

Dylan knew, without a shadow of a doubt in that moment, that this was all his fault. Courtney was never going to change. No, he'd always known that about her, and still he let her get involved in Ben's life again. He could have put his foot down, hired a damn good lawyer, and rode out whatever legal circus she tried to create, but instead, he'd taken the path of least resistance. He'd brought her back into Ben's life, and she was just going to walk back on out like it was nothing. And the only person who would pay the price was Ben.

"Okay, we'll take that into consideration," the Sheriff said. "Now, I'll need you both with me while we get our team up to speed. Come along now."

Courtney trudged after the Sheriff, and Dylan turned to look at Faye, who was leaning against the donation table, her brow creased with worry. When she saw Dylan looking at her, she went to him, wrapping her arms around his neck in a tight hug. After a moment, she pulled back.

"How can I help?" she asked. "Do you want me to come with you?"

"No," he said, without any hesitation. Her brows knit together, and he continued, "I just mean, it's alright. It might make more sense for you to stay here, anyway. In case he comes back."

"Right, of course," she said. After a moment, she added, "Dylan, it's going to be fine. They're going to find him."

"I know," he said. The truth was, he didn't know. He just didn't want to think about the possibility of the alternative. "I should get going."

"Okay."

He ran to catch up with Courtney and the Sheriff, noticing how dark it had gotten all of a sudden. The temperature had dropped with the sun gone, and Dylan could see his breath in front of him. His hands started to sting, and he rubbed them together, trying to warm them He only hoped they found Ben soon, before it got even colder outside. He couldn't bear to think of his son alone and freezing.

FAYE WATCHED HIM GO, feeling totally and utterly helpless. A slight wind had kicked up, sending a shiver through her, and she wrapped her arms a little tighter around herself. She hated to think of Ben all alone in this cold, and hoped that the Sheriff and his team would find him soon.

She stood by the donation table, her legs restless and wanting to walk, wanting to help find Ben. She didn't want to just stand around, although she knew it was important to have a familiar face around in case he did come back. A few people had stopped by her table to let her know that they'd keep an eye out for Ben, too, and the feeling of helplessness had only intensified. *They* were even doing more to find Ben than she was just standing around. She noticed Chloe walking toward her with David, and was relieved to see her friend in the midst of all the chaos. She gave her a much-needed hug.

"It's going to be fine," Chloe said, shooting a look at David, who nodded his head emphatically.

"They're going to find him in no time, there are a ton of people out searching right now," he said.

"I feel completely useless just waiting here, but Dylan thought someone should be here in case Ben came back," Faye explained. "I want to be out there looking, too. I want to help."

Chloe thought for a moment, then grabbed Faye's hand. "David will wait here. We will go help with the search."

Faye looked hopefully at David. "Oh, would you? Do you mind?" she asked, and David shook his head.

"Go ahead," he said. "I'll wait here in case he comes back, and if he does, I'll call Chloe right away."

Chloe beamed at him, then tugged Faye along. They joined a small group of searchers walking toward the North End of the village, away from the lake and toward the school. Among the group was Nancy Harding, who owned a little antique shop in the village, and Cynthia Whitfield, who ran the town's one and only hair salon. Ethel Saperstein, one of the town's oldest, and feistiest, residents, plodded along in the front of the pack with her cane and tall gray beehive hairdo, leading the charge.

"Sure is cold out tonight," Nancy said, pulling her coat a little tighter around herself. "Let's all keep our eyes peeled!"

Cynthia, who definitely was not dressed for the occasion in a stylish, but not very warm-looking camel-colored shawl, chattered alongside her. "This is the sort of weather that makes you want to curl up next to the fire with a good book," she said longingly. "Poor Ben."

Faye stopped abruptly, Cynthia's words reverberating in her head. *With a good book*. She grabbed Chloe's arm, and Chloe gave her a confused look as they stopped in the middle of the sidewalk, the rest of the group continuing on.

"Faye, what is it?"

"I think I know where he might have gone," she told her. She yanked Chloe forward, breaking into a jog. "Come on!"

Chapter Fifteen

They made it to the elementary school a few minutes later, Chloe bending over with her hands on her knees as she wheezed, trying to catch her breath. She looked around, and then at Faye, and incredulous look on her face.

"A little boy ran away, and you think he went to *school*?" Chloe chided. "Were you never a kid once?"

Faye rolled her eyes, and tugged her friend forward. "Come on!"

They slipped in through the front doors and quietly tiptoed down the dimly lit hallways. Most of the classroom doors were closed, the classrooms dark behind them.

"Faye, it's dark, there's nobody in here," Chloe said. "I don't think this is the right place."

"Just trust me," Faye said, taking a sharp right turn, and stopping at the end of a hallway. At the other end, light spilled out of one of the classrooms, bathing the hallway in pale, yellow light. She turned to look at Chloe. "I left my lights on and my door unlocked so we could bring the donations back after the Festival," she said, starting down the hallway toward the classroom. Chloe followed behind her.

The closer she got, the more sure she felt that Ben would be here. Courtney had said he might have been upset, and Faye could think of one thing she loved to do to escape when she was sad. She was fairly certain that Ben did, too.

She quietly entered her classroom, and stopped just inside the doorway, exhaling a sigh of relief. Underneath the window, curled up on a bean-bag chair next to the bookshelves, sound asleep, with *The Velveteen Rabbit* lying open next to him, was Ben.

Chloe put a hand to her chest and mouthed *Thank God*, then gave Faye's arm a squeeze. Faye tiptoed over to Ben and gently shook him awake. His eyes fluttered open sleepily, and he sat up, looking around as if trying to remember where he was.

"Hi, Miss Parker," he said, before his mouth stretched into a big yawn.

"Hi, Ben," she said, sitting down on the beanbag chair next to him. "Have you been here this whole time?" she asked, and he looked at the floor, his cheeks turning pink. He nodded.

"Am I in trouble?" he asked, and Faye chuckled.

"No, Ben. You're not in trouble. But everyone was very worried about you," she said. He looked up at her, his eyes growing watery. "Why didn't you tell anyone where you were going?"

He looked down again. "Because I was mad."

"Mad about what?" she asked.

"My mom's going to leave again," he said. He sniffled, and Faye's heart broke for the little boy. She put an arm around him and pulled him onto her lap.

"You don't know that," she said, but Ben just shrugged.

"I heard her talking," he sighed. "She said so."

"Well no matter what, I promise it's going to be alright," she told him. She couldn't speak for what Courtney would do, and she didn't want to make any promises to Ben that she couldn't keep. What she could promise, however, was to be there for him if he needed her. "You can read a book from the class library whenever you want, okay?"

He gave her a tiny smile. "Okay."

"Now, we should really get you back to your mom and dad. They're really worried," Faye told him, and the smile disappeared, replaced with something Faye was all too used to seeing in her students - a fear of getting in trouble.

The three of them left the school together and made their way back to where the Festival was winding down. To make sure he didn't have to worry any longer than necessary, Faye sent Dylan a text letting him know that she'd found Ben, where she had found him, and that she and Ben would be meeting up with them shortly He'd responded with *Thank God!*, and told her that he and Courtney would meet them by the donations table.

When they got there, the look of relief on Dylan's face nearly brought Faye to tears. Chloe went to David, and they began to round up the donations to bring over to the school. Ben launched himself at his father and Dylan picked him up, hugging him close and burying his face in his hair. Courtney ran to them, planting kisses all over Ben's head and sniffling as more tears streamed down her cheeks. Faye watched them, the happiness she felt at their reunion mixing with a feeling she couldn't quite define. She felt out of place all of the sudden, like she was intruding. For some reason, watching Dylan with Ben and Courtney, looking like a family - she felt itchy and uncomfortable, like she needed to get out of there. Dylan put Ben down and met her gaze, and the usual butterflies she felt were overshadowed by something else, something she didn't want to admit in the middle of what should have been a happy moment. She felt *envy*.

He strode over to her and wrapped her in a hug, the strength and warmth of his body surrounding her. She should have felt comforted, and she did, to an extent. But she couldn't shake the churning in the pit of her stomach. He released her, and suddenly she felt bare and exposed.

"Thank you, Faye," he murmured, and she nodded her head, unsure of what to say. *You're welcome?* No, it just didn't seem to fit. Instead, she gave him a weary smile, her eyes searching for something, anything in his that might reassure her.

They stood in silence for what felt like an eternity.

"Chloe and David are going to bring the donations to the school," she said. "I have to go lock up, but maybe when I'm done, and you get Ben home and settled, I could stop by for a little while?"

Dylan's smile faded, and the churning in her stomach worsened. He looked at his shoes, and Faye felt her cheeks growing hot.

"I'm not sure," he said, running a hand through his hair. "I just - I think maybe tonight isn't a good night. Ben's upset, and Courtney's a wreck, and I think I should just be with my family for right now."

His family. Even though she knew exactly what he meant, the words cut through her life a knife. Of course he wanted to be with Ben and Courtney after what they'd just gone through, how stupid could she possibly be? Why would she think that she had any right to intrude on a night like tonight? She stood up straighter, hoping to hide her disappointment.

"Of course," she said. "I completely understand. Please tell Ben I'm glad he's safe."

She started to walk away, fighting back the tears that stung her eyes and the embarrassment that stung her pride.

"Faye!" he called after her, and she looked back at him, feeling foolish at how her heart raced whenever he said her name. He held her gaze for a moment, her heart pounding in her chest. "I'll call you," he said, and she nodded, before quickly turning away and heading to her car. When she finally slid into the driver's seat, she let the tears come, all the conflicting emotions she felt pouring out of her into the cold, still night.

Chapter Sixteen

Chloe sat down across from Faye and slid her large cappuccino to her, watching with marked concern as she took a long sip. Aside from work, Faye had been holed up inside her house for the last few days feeling sorry for herself. Dylan hadn't called. In fact, she hadn't heard from him at all. She'd broken down the previous night after one too many glasses of red wine and had texted him, and his response had only made her feel worse.

I just can't have any distractions right now. I need to focus on Ben. I'm sorry.

She hadn't seen Courtney around, but she knew from reading the internet gossip that she was still in Pine Grove. Yes, the tabloids were fascinated with the fact that Courtney had gone "off the grid" in a small town on the other side of the country, coincidentally the same town where her famous snowboarder ex-boyfriend was living. All of cyberspace was speculating that the pair were getting back together. *Getting Back Together for the Kid?* one headline read. *Long Lost Love Rekindled?* read another. Reading them made her nauseous, but she couldn't stop. She just wanted an inkling, something, *anything* that might tell her what he was up to. Christmas was in two days, and they'd be back to school before they knew it. She would surely see Dylan then. But the waiting, and the wondering, were killing her.

"If you're going to keep sulking like this, I'm going to start spiking these," Chloe said, motioning to Faye's coffee. "Seriously, I hate seeing you like this."

"Like what?"

"Like. . . Someone just ran over your puppy. Come on, it's almost Christmas. You can't be sad at Christmas."

Faye smiled, appreciating that her friend wanted to cheer her up. She supposed she should be grateful that things with Dylan hadn't gone any farther than they did. If experience had taught her anything, it was that just because she felt something about someone, didn't always mean they returned those feelings. She'd learned that with Peter, after spending years thinking he loved her just as much as she loved him. At least with Dylan, she'd learned quickly and without too much investment that it wasn't going to work.

"I bought Ben a Christmas present," she said, feeling silly even uttering it out loud. "A book I thought he might like. Now it just seems. . . weird."

"I think you should still give it to him," Chloe said, taking a sip of her own coffee. "Just because Dylan is an idiot doesn't mean Ben should have to suffer."

Faye rolled her eyes and laughed, despite how miserable she felt.

"I got the final tally on the donations," Faye said, trying to change the subject. "We doubled last year's donations. We were able to furnish the entire neighboring school district with supplies."

"I know!" Chloe gushed. "I saw the article they did in the Syracuse Times." The moment Chloe mentioned the article, her face went white as a sheet. "Oh, crap. I'm so sorry."

"It's fine," Faye said. "The article really helped get the word out. We had a ton of donations mailed in the last few days."

She didn't want to think about the part Dylan probably played in it all. His mere presence had brought a ton more traffic to the donation table at the Festival than she'd ever seen before. The article also hadn't wasted the opportunity to capitalize on Dylan's involvement, and while it had likely drawn a larger readership for the newspaper, it had definitely influenced the influx of donations they'd received by mail. Like it or not, she couldn't deny Dylan had played a huge role in the success of supply drive.

"Okay, well I want you to stop sulking and get excited. We're going to do Christmas Eve brunch, and I will make sure there are enough mimosas that Dylan Andersen is nothing but a distant, fleeting memory," Chloe said. Just then, the bell above the door to the cafe jingled, and a small crowd of people walked into the cafe and formed a line at the register. Chloe stood up, draining her coffee cup, and giving Faye a quick hug. "Duty calls," she said. "I'll see you tomorrow!"

She bounded off behind the counter, and Faye put on her coat and gathered her things. She swung her bag over her shoulder, catching a glimpse of the book she'd gotten for Ben, all wrapped up in Christmas paper, nestled inside. She thought about what Chloe had said, and realized she was right - Ben still deserved the gift, regardless of what was happening - or *not* happening - between her and Dylan.

Chugging the rest of her coffee, she decided the right thing to do was to act like a rational, mature adult and deliver the gift. She wouldn't stay and chit chat, wouldn't do anything but drop off the gift for Ben and then leave. She would not make it awkward or uncomfortable.

When she pulled up outside of Dylan's house, she had to sit for a moment to calm her nerves. She took a few deep, calming breaths, and then grabbed the wrapped book out of her bag and walked up to the front door. She knocked three times, and waited.

The door swung open, and Dylan stood in the doorway, his eyes growing wide when he saw Faye.

"Hi," he said, swallowing hard.

"Hello," Faye said. "I'm sorry to come by without calling first, is now a bad time?"

"No, not at all," he said. "What's, um, what's up?"

She held up the book, feeling her cheeks getting red. "I brought this for Ben. Just a small gift for Christmas."

She handed it to him, and he took it, looking at her with an intensity that gave her chills. They stood there on the porch, his gaze locked on hers for what felt like an eternity until he cleared his throat looked down at his shoes.

"So, how are you?" he asked, his face sheepish.

"I'm fine," she replied, perhaps a little too quickly. "And you?"

"I'm good," he said. She heard the sound of footsteps in the house behind him, and Courtney appeared in the doorway. She saw Faye, and only a brief flicker of emotion passed across her face. If she felt any kind of way about Faye being there, she was doing her best to hide it.

"Well, tell Ben Merry Christmas for me," she said, before whirling around and practically running back to her car. She didn't wait for Dylan to say anything. She didn't even give him a last look. She inhaled a deep breath when she got to her car, and without even another glance back, took off back home.

Dylan watched her go, holding the gift she'd dropped off in his hand, a sudden tightness squeezing his chest. He could feel Courtney standing behind him, had heard her approach, but waited until Faye's car was long gone before he turned around to face her. Courtney's lips were pursed together, her eyes narrowed at him, and he gulped.

"You are many things, Dylan, but an idiot isn't one of them," she said, stalking into the kitchen where her bags stood packed next to the kitchen table. Dylan wasn't happy that Courtney leaving would hurt Ben, but he had to admit, he was happy his guest room would finally be empty again. He was tired of Courtney walking around like she owned the place, a constant, disapproving glare on her face at his choice of decor and furnishings. He cocked an eyebrow at her.

"That might be the nicest thing you've ever said to me," he jeered.

"What's that?" she asked, nodding to the gift in his hand. Dylan smirked.

"Faye brought it for Ben," he told her, walking over, and setting it on top of the kitchen table. He looked up Courtney, whose face was unreadable. "He's going to miss you, ya know."

The corner of her mouth twitched. "I know. I'm going to miss him, too."

Dylan sat down at the table and massaged his temples. "You don't *have* to go," he said. "I'd rather you didn't stay in *my house*, but you could find a place in Pine Grove that's close by."

She smiled, and shook her head. "I have to go," she murmured. "I know how that sounds, but you know me. I love Ben, and I will miss him, but I'm not cut out for. . ." She looked around and threw her hands up. "This! At least not long term."

"But you will come back, right?" Dylan asked. "Ben likes having you around, and I know he'd be devastated to lose his mom again."

"I know," she said, "and I will visit, I promise. The London campaign should only be a few weeks, so I'll come back once that's finished for a while. I'll try and see Ben a few days a month and maybe, once we're in a better place, he could come visit me some time."

Dylan gave her a pointed look. "We'll see."

She put her hands up in front of her. "I know, I know."

Ben padded down the stairs and into the kitchen, a solemn look on his face. Dylan frowned, knowing that the aftermath of Courtney leaving would be something he'd have to deal with for a long time coming. He watched as Courtney knelt down next to Ben and gave him a hug, telling him how she'd be back in a few weeks, and that they would see much, much more of each other. When she stood up, she turned toward Dylan.

"Listen," she said, putting her hands on her hips. "I see the way you look at her, Dylan. You'd be an idiot to let her get away."

"Stop," Dylan said, turning away from her so she couldn't see the pain in his eyes. "I don't need the distraction right now. I need to focus on Ben."

"You can focus on Ben while still letting yourself have a *life*, Dylan. You don't have to give everything up."

"No, no I can't. You might be able to just walk away, but I'm his father and I have to be there to protect him. Last time I only thought about myself, and look what happened! He was gone, Courtney. I can't ever let that happen again."

She frowned, and grabbed his hand in hers. He looked at her, confused by the surprisingly tender gesture. Her face softened as she spoke.

"Nothing about that day was your fault, Dylan. It was mine. And Ben is fine, you didn't do anything wrong. Don't let this one get away. You deserve to be happy, and she makes you happy, Dylan. It's obvious."

He closed his eyes, inhaling a deep breath and holding it in for a beat. When he opened them, she was looking at him still, her face full of concern.

"I'm afraid I already screwed it up," he said.

"You won't know unless you try."

She collected her bags walked to the door, kneeling down to give Ben one last hug and kiss. She stood up, and gave Dylan a kiss on the cheek.

"Don't let her get away," she said. Then, a devious grin crossed her face. "Or I'll tell Martin you're thinking about competing again. You don't want that, do you?"

Dylan shook his head. "No, I suppose I don't."

She winked at him, and then disappeared out the front door. When she was gone, he turned around and rested his back against the door, his stomach churning. He knew that Courtney was right. What he and Faye had shared, no matter how brief it was, had been different from anything he'd ever experienced before. He'd known it was special, and frankly, that scared the crap out of him. But after what he'd said to her? Calling her a distraction? He didn't know if she would forgive him for that, let alone speak to him again. He wouldn't blame her if she didn't.

You won't know unless you try. Courtney's words resounded in his head, and he looked down at Ben, who was watching him expectantly.

"Get your shoes, Ben."

"Where are we going?"

He knelt down in front of his son, ruffling his blond hair.

"Daddy has an errand to run."

Chapter Seventeen

Chloe showed up to Faye's house around noon, a bottle of champagne and a box of assorted pastries in hand. It had started to snow, big, fat flakes blanketing the ground and casting a serene silence in the air. Faye had desperately wanted a white Christmas, and it looked like she just might get it.

She put on a pot of coffee while Chloe rifled through Faye's DVD collection, pulling out a handful of Christmas cult classics and bringing them over to the kitchen.

"Alright, *White Christmas, A Charlie Brown Christmas,* or *The Sound of Music?*" Chloe asked. Faye spun around, giving her friend a cross-eyed look.

"*The Sound of Music?* Is that even a Christmas movie?" she asked, and Chloe scoffed.

"I can't believe you just asked me that. *The Sound of Music* is an all-occasions kind of film."

"Alright, well why don't we try *White Christmas* first, and we can see how we feel after that," Faye said, and Chloe laughed. She bounded back into the living room, and Faye could hear the DVD player opening as she loaded the disc. Faye pulled two mugs down from the cabinet, and was about to fill them with coffee, when there was a knock at the door.

She and Chloe exchanged a look, and Faye felt her stomach twist into a knot. She sucked in a breath and walked to the door, Chloe creeping up behind her to see who was at the door. Her pulse quickened as she grasped the door handle, and she hesitated for a moment before pulling it open.

One her doorstep stood Dylan and Ben, both wearing elaborate Christmas sweaters under their coats, their hair covered in snow. She met Dylan's gaze, her heart beating like a drum as he flashed her one of his famous, captivating smiles. She fought the urge to melt into a puddle right then and there.

"Hello, Faye," he said, the sound of her name in that rich, velvety voice sending shivers up her spine.

"Hi," she breathed, glancing back over her shoulder at Chloe, who gave her a look that said *well, what are you waiting for?* She smiled nervously at Dylan, stumbling over the words she wanted to say. "Would you, um, do you want to come inside?" she asked, and he smiled even wider.

"Sure, thank you."

He and Ben stepped inside, and Dylan stopped when he saw Chloe in the kitchen, sipping from a mug of coffee.

"I'm sorry," he said, "I didn't realize you had company."

Chloe waved her free hand in the air. "Pretend I'm not even here."

Faye bit back the laughter than was bubbling up inside of her, which wasn't difficult when his gaze traveled back to rest on her. Her breath hitched when he took a few steps closer, his eyes laser-locked on hers, that familiar masculine confidence practically radiating from him as she tried to steady her breathing.

"I need to apologize," he said, taking another step closer. "I pushed you away because I was scared of how easy it was to be with you. To trust you." He took another yet step closer, and Faye swore she could feel her pulse all the way down to her toes. He reached out his hand and brushed her fingers, tangling them in his. "To fall for you," he continued. "I've been so worried about giving Ben a normal life, I forgot that I'm allowed to have one, too. A life with happiness, friendships. . ." He stepped even closer, until there were just a few inches between them. "With love."

She wasn't even sure she was breathing anymore. Without breaking eye contact, he reached out his hand toward Ben, who handed him a box. A red and silver tin box, with Christmas trees and snowmen and familiar script on the lid. Tears stung the back of her eyes as he handed her the box of ribbon candy. She took it, her hands shaking, a smile tugging at the corners of her lips. He lifted his hand to her face, brushing his fingers against her cheek, his thumb trailing across her jawline, weaving it's way over her bottom lip until she was completely engulfed in tingles from head to toe.

"I don't know if I can promise I won't screw up again. Or that some tabloid magazine won't make us front page news. But I can promise to love you for as long as you love me, and then longer."

She held up the box, grinning from ear to ear. "Even if I have lots and lots of cavities?" she asked, earning her another fabulous smile. He snatched the box back and gave it to Ben, then closed the few inches between them.

"No matter what," he murmured, before lowering his head and brushing his lips on hers. He was tentative at first, as if seeing how she would react. His hands found her waist, while hers slipped over his shoulders and around his neck, the need in his kiss burning so hot, she might as well have been on fire. They stood there in the foyer, lost in the passion of the moment, when the sound of someone clearing their throat startled them both.

Faye whipped her head toward the kitchen, where Chloe was holding the bottle of champagne in one hand, her other poised on the cork. She pulled it, and a loud *Pop!* echoed throughout the room, bubbles shooting out the top and spilling over the bottle like a Prosecco volcano.

"Who wants a mimosa?" Chloe asked, as they all dissolved into laughter, Faye still in Dylan's arms. Their eyes met, and he didn't have to say anything for her to understand how he felt in that moment. Like everything she needed in the world was right here.

"Merry Christmas, Faye," he murmured, while the clink of Chloe pulling champagne flutes out of the cabinet chimed behind them. She saw Ben with her in the kitchen, peering at the box of pastries while Chloe rattled off her favorites.

She turned back to Dylan and leaned in, kissing him again.

"Merry Christmas."

About the Author

Author of contemporary romance, Jessica Thorn brings to life stories full of heart with just enough heat, that tug on your heartstrings, quicken your pulse, and bring a massive smile to your face.

Follow her on Facebook at:

https://www.facebook.com/jessicathornbooks

Visit her website at www.jessicathornbooks.com

To stay up to date on new releases and get exclusive author content, subscribe to her newsletter at:

https://jessicathornbooks.ck.page/bc03070198

Made in United States
Orlando, FL
18 January 2022